**Praise for the novels of *New York Times* and
USA TODAY bestselling author
DIANA PALMER**

"Palmer demonstrates, yet again, why she's the
queen of desperado quests for justice and true love."
—*Publishers Weekly* on *Dangerous*

"The popular Palmer has penned another winning
novel, a perfect blend of romance and suspense."
—*Booklist* on *Lawman*

"This is a fascinating story... It's nice to have a hero
wise enough to know when he can't do things alone
and willing to accept help when he needs it.
There is pleasure to be found in the nice sense of
family this tale imparts."
—*RT Book Reviews* on *Wyoming Bold*

"Diana Palmer is a mesmerizing storyteller who
captures the essence of what a romance should be."
—*Affaire de Coeur*

"Readers will be moved by this tale of revenge
and justice, grief and healing."
—*Booklist* on *Dangerous*

Dear Reader,

I didn't start out to write another mercenary book. It might help if I explain how I write. I'll be watching a movie or reading a book or playing games on my computer when something flashes into my mind. Usually it's a person with some specific background. Mostly it's a man. I stop whatever I'm doing and try to see who he is and where he is and why he's there. Then I'll see another person, this time a woman. I see them exactly as I'll describe them later in a book.

As I try to figure out what point they've reached in their individual lives, I'll see glimpses of their pasts, where they came from, who their people are. By this point, I'm totally intrigued with them. It becomes like watching a movie. I write down what I see as fast as I can, until I get to the end of the book. I might point out that this is a particularly difficult way to do a book, because if I get sick and can't work, a whole book may pass right through my brain without stopping for the computer. I have, in fact, lost two books that way over the years.

It's the most mysterious process you can imagine. All writers have their individual writing methods. Some do a page or two a day. Others, like me, start a book and drive the family crazy because they can't be bothered to do normal things until it's finished. So I wrote a book about a mercenary because that's what I saw when Gabriel Brandon's face came into my mind. I like the result. I hope you do, too.

Diana Palmer

DIANA PALMER

Texas
BORN

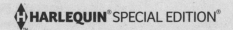

HARLEQUIN® SPECIAL EDITION®

Recycling programs
for this product may
not exist in your area.

ISBN-13: 978-0-373-65841-1

TEXAS BORN

Printed in U.S.A.

Also available from Diana Palmer

Other books in the Morcai Battalion series

And coming soon

For our friends Cynthia Burton and Terry Sosebee

Chapter One

Michelle Godfrey felt the dust of the unpaved road all over her jeans. She couldn't really see her pants. Her eyes were full of hot tears. It was just one more argument, one more heartache.

Her stepmother, Roberta, was determined to sell off everything her father had owned. He'd only been dead for three weeks. Roberta had wanted to bury him in a plain pine box with no flowers, not even a church service. Michelle had dared her stepmother's hot temper and appealed to the funeral director.

The kindly man, a friend of her father's, had pointed out to Roberta that Comanche Wells, Texas, was a very small community. It would not sit well with the locals if Roberta, whom most considered an outsider, was disrespectful of the late Alan Godfrey's wishes that he be buried in the Methodist church cemetery beside his first wife. The funeral director was soft-spoken but eloquent.

He also pointed out that the money Roberta would save with her so-called economy plans, would be a very small amount compared to the outrage she would provoke. If she planned to continue living in Jacobs County, many doors would close to her.

Roberta was irritated at the comment, but she had a shrewd mind. It wouldn't do to make people mad when she had many things to dispose of on the local market, including some cattle that had belonged to her late husband.

She gave in, with ill grace, and left the arrangements to Michelle. But she got even. After the funeral, she gathered up Alan's personal items while Michelle was at school and sent them all to the landfill, including his clothes and any jewelry that wasn't marketable.

Michelle had collapsed in tears. That is, until she saw her stepmother's wicked smile. At that point, she dried her eyes. It was too late to do anything. But one day, she promised herself, when she was grown and no longer under the woman's guardianship, there would be a reckoning.

Two weeks after the funeral, Roberta came under fire from Michelle's soft-spoken minister. He drove up in front of the house in a flashy red older convertible, an odd choice of car for a man of the cloth, Michelle thought. But then, Reverend Blair was a different sort of preacher.

She'd let him in, offered him coffee, which he refused politely. Roberta, curious because they never had visitors, came out of her room and stopped short when she saw Jake Blair.

He greeted her. He even smiled. They'd missed Michelle at services for the past two weeks. He just wanted to make sure everything was all right. Michelle didn't reply. Roberta looked guilty. There was this strange rumor he'd heard, he continued, that Roberta was preventing her stepdaughter from attending church services. He smiled when he said it, but there was something about him that was strangely chilling for a religious man. His eyes, ice-blue, had a look that Roberta recognized from her youth, spent following her father around the casinos in Las Vegas, where he made his living. Some of the patrons had that same penetrating gaze. It was dangerous.

"But of course, we didn't think the rumor was true," Jake Blair continued with that smile that accompanied the unblinking blue stare. "It isn't, is it?"

Roberta forced a smile. "Um, of course not." She faltered, with a nervous little laugh. "She can go whenever she likes."

"You might consider coming with her," Jake commented. "We welcome new members in our congregation."

"Me, in a church?" She burst out laughing, until she saw the two bland faces watching her. She sounded defensive when she added, "I don't go to church. I don't believe in all that stuff."

Jake raised an eyebrow. He smiled to himself, as if at some private joke. "At some point in your life, I assure you, your beliefs may change."

"Unlikely," she said stiffly.

He sighed. "As you wish. Then you won't mind if my daughter, Carlie, comes by to pick Michelle up for services on Sunday, I take it?"

Roberta ground her teeth together. Obviously the minister knew that since Michelle couldn't drive, Roberta had been refusing to get up and drive her to church. She almost refused. Then she realized that it would mean she could have Bert over without having to watch for her stepdaughter every second. She pursed her lips. "Of course not," she assured him. "I don't mind at all."

"Wonderful. I'll have Carlie fetch you in time for Sunday school each week and bring you home after church, Michelle. Will that work for you?"

Michelle's sad face lit up. Her gray eyes were large and beautiful. She had pale blond hair and a flawless, lovely complexion. She was as fair as Roberta was dark. Jake got to his feet. He smiled down at Michelle.

"Thanks, Reverend Blair," she said in her soft, husky voice, and smiled at him with genuine affection.

"You're quite welcome."

She walked him out. Roberta didn't offer.

He turned at the steps and lowered his voice. "If you ever need help, you know where we are," he said, and he wasn't smiling.

She sighed. "It's just until graduation. Only a few more months," she said quietly. "I'll work hard to get a scholarship so I can go to college. I have one picked out in San Antonio."

He cocked his head. "What do you want to do?"

Her face brightened. "I want to write. I want to be a reporter."

He laughed. "Not much money in that, you know. Of course, you could go and talk to Minette Carson. She runs the local newspaper."

She flushed. "Yes, sir," she said politely, "I already did. She was the one who recommended that I go to college and major in journalism. She said working for a magazine, even a digital one, was the way to go. She's very kind."

"She is. And so is her husband," he added, referring to Jacobs County sheriff Hayes Carson.

"I don't really know him. Except he brought his iguana to school a few years ago. That was really fascinating." She laughed.

Jake just nodded. "Well, I'll get back. Let me know if you need anything."

"I will. Thank you."

"Your father was a good man," he added. "It hurt all of us to lose him. He was one of the best emergency-room doctors we ever had in Jacobs County, even though he was only able to work for a few months before his illness forced him to quit."

She smiled sadly. "It was a hard way to go, for a doctor," she replied. "He knew all about his prognosis and he explained to me how things would be. He said if he hadn't been so stubborn, if he'd had the tests sooner, they might have caught the cancer in time."

"Young lady," Jake said softly, "things happen the way they're meant to. There's a plan to everything that happens in life, even if we don't see it."

"That's what I think, too. Thank you for talking to her," she added hesitantly. "She wouldn't let me learn how to drive, and Dad was too sick to teach me. I don't really think she'd let me borrow the car, even if I could drive. She wouldn't get up early for anything, especially on a Sunday. So I had no way to get to church. I've missed it."

"I wish you'd talked to me sooner," he said, and smiled. "Never mind. Things happen in their own time."

She looked up into his blue eyes. "Does it…get better? Life, I mean?" she asked with the misery of someone who'd landed in a hard place and saw no way out.

He drew in a long breath. "You'll soon have more control over the things that happen to you," he replied. "Life is a test, Michelle. We walk through fire. But there are rewards. Every pain brings a pleasure."

"Thanks."

He chuckled. "Don't let her get you down."

"I'm trying."

"And if you need help, don't hold back." His eyes narrowed and there was something a little chilling in them. "I have yet to meet a person who frightens me."

She burst out laughing. "I noticed. She's a horror, but she was really nice to you!"

"Sensible people are." He smiled like an angel. "See you."

He went down the steps two at a time. He was a tall man, very fit, and he walked with a very odd gait, light and almost soundless, as he went to his car. The vehicle wasn't new, but it had some kind of big engine in it. He started it and wheeled out into the road with a skill and smoothness that she envied. She wondered if she'd ever learn to drive.

She went back into the house, resigned to several minutes of absolute misery.

"You set that man on me!" Roberta raged. "You went over my head when I told you I didn't want you to bother with that stupid church stuff!"

"I like going to church. Why should you mind? It isn't hurting you...."

"Dinner was always late when you went, when your father was alive," the brunette said angrily. "I had to take care of him. So messy." She made a face. In fact, Roberta had never done a thing for her husband. She left it all to Michelle. "And I had to try to cook. I hate cooking. I'm not doing it. That's your job. So you'll make dinner before you go to church and you can eat when you get home, but I'm not waiting an extra hour to sit down to a meal!"

"I'll do it," Michelle said, averting her eyes.

"See that you do! And the house had better be spotless, or I won't let you go!"

She was bluffing. Michelle knew it. She was unsettled by the Reverend Blair. That amused Michelle, but she didn't dare let it show.

"Can I go to my room now?" she asked quietly.

Roberta made a face. "Do what you please." She primped at the hall mirror. "I'm going out. Bert's taking me to dinner up in San Antonio. I'll be very late," she added. She gave Michelle a worldly, patronizing laugh. "You wouldn't know what to do with a man, you little prude."

Michelle stiffened. It was the same old song and dance. Roberta thought Michelle was backward and stupid.

"Oh, go on to your room," she muttered. That wide-eyed, resigned look was irritating.

Michelle went without another word.

She sat up late, studying. She had to make the best grades she could, so that she could get a scholarship. Her father had left her a little money, but her stepmother had control of it until she was of legal age. Probably by then there wouldn't be a penny left.

Her father hadn't been lucid at the end because of the massive doses of painkillers he had to take for his condition. Roberta had influenced the way he set up his will, and it had been her own personal attorney who'd drawn it up for her father's signature. Michelle was certain that he hadn't meant to leave her so little. But she couldn't contest it. She wasn't even out of high school.

It was hard, she thought, to be under someone's thumb and unable to do anything you wanted to do. Roberta was always after her about something. She made fun of her, ridiculed her conservative clothes, made her life a daily misery. But the reverend was right. One day, she'd be out of this. She'd have her own place, and she wouldn't have to ask Roberta even for lunch money, which was demeaning enough.

She heard a truck go along the road, and glanced out to see a big black pickup truck pass by. So he was back. Their closest neighbor was Gabriel Brandon. Michelle knew who he was.

She'd seen him for the first time two years ago, the last summer she'd spent with her grandfather and grandmother before their deaths. They'd lived in this very house, the one her father had inherited. She'd gone to town with her grandfather to get medicine for a sick calf. The owner of the store had been talking to a man, a very handsome man who'd just moved down the road from them.

He was very tall, muscular, without it being obvious, and he had the most beautiful liquid black eyes she'd ever seen. He was built like a rodeo cowboy. He had thick, jet-black hair and a face off of a movie poster. He was the most gorgeous man she'd ever seen in her life.

He'd caught her staring at him and he'd laughed. She'd never forgotten how that transformed his hard face. It had melted her. She'd flushed and averted her eyes and almost run out of the store afterward. She'd embarrassed herself by staring. But he was very good-looking, after all—he must be used to women staring at him.

She'd asked her grandfather about him. He hadn't said much, only that the man was working for Eb Scott, who owned a ranch near Jacobsville. Brandon was rather mysterious, too, her grandfather had mused, and people were curious about him. He wasn't married. He had a sister who visited him from time to time.

Michelle's grandfather had chided her for her interest. At fifteen, he'd reminded her, she was much too young to be interested in men. She'd agreed out loud. But privately she thought that that Mr. Brandon was absolutely gorgeous, and most girls would have stared at him.

By comparison, Roberta's friend, Bert, always looked greasy, as if he never washed his hair. Michelle couldn't stand him. He looked at her in a way that made her skin crawl and he was always trying to touch her. She'd jerked away from him once, when he'd tried to ruffle her hair, and he made a big joke of it. But his eyes weren't laughing.

He made her uncomfortable, and she tried to stay out of his way. It would have been all right if he and Roberta didn't flaunt their affair. Michelle came home from school one Monday to find them on the sofa together, half-dressed and sweaty. Roberta had almost doubled up with laughter at the look she got from her stepdaughter as she lay half across Bert, wearing nothing but a lacy black slip.

"And what are you staring at, you little prude?" Roberta had demanded. "Did you think I'd put on black clothes and abandon men for life because your father died?"

"He's only been dead two weeks," Michelle had pointed out with choking pride.

"So what? He wasn't even that good in bed before he got sick," she scoffed. "We lived in San Antonio and he had a wonderful practice, he was making loads of money as a cardiologist. Then he gets diagnosed with terminal cancer and decides overnight to pull up stakes and move to this flea-bitten wreck of a town where he sets up a free clinic on weekends and lives on his pension and his investments! Which evaporated in less than a year, thanks to his medical bills," she added haughtily. "I thought he was rich…!"

"Yes, that's why you married him," Michelle said under her breath.

"That's the only reason I did marry him," she muttered, sitting up to light a cigarette and blow smoke in Michelle's direction.

She coughed. "Daddy wouldn't let you smoke in the house," she said accusingly.

"Well, Daddy's dead, isn't he?" Roberta said pointedly, and she smiled.

"We could make it a threesome, if you like," Bert offered, sitting up with his shirt half-off.

Michelle's expression was eloquent. "If I speak to my minister…"

"Shut up, Bert!" Roberta said shortly, and her eyes dared him to say another word. She looked back at Michelle with cold eyes and got to her feet. "Come on, Bert, let's go to your place." She grabbed him by the hand and had led him to the bedroom. Apparently their clothes were in there.

Disgusted beyond measure, Michelle went into her room and locked the door.

She could hear them arguing. A few minutes later they came back out.

"I won't be here for dinner," Roberta said.

Michelle didn't reply.

"Little torment," Roberta grumbled. "She's always watching, always so pure and unblemished," she added harshly.

"I could take care of that," Bert said.

"Shut up!" Roberta said again. "Come on, Bert!"

Michelle could feel herself flushing with anger as she heard them go out the door. Roberta slammed it behind her.

Michelle had peeked out the curtains and watched them climb into Bert's low-slung car. He pulled out into the road.

She closed the curtains with a sigh of pure relief. Nobody knew what a hell those two made of her life. She had no peace. Apparently Roberta had been seeing Bert for some time, because they were obviously obsessed with each other. But it had come as a shock to walk in the door and find them kissing the day after Michelle's father was buried, to say nothing of what she'd just seen.

The days since then had been tense and uncomfortable. The two of them made fun of Michelle, ridiculed the way she dressed, the way she thought. And Roberta was full of petty comments about Michelle's father and the illness that had killed him. Roberta had never even gone to the hospital. It had been Michelle who'd sat with him until he slipped away, peacefully, in his sleep.

She lay on her back and looked at the ceiling. It was only a few months until graduation. She made very good grades. She hoped Marist College in San Antonio would take her. She'd already applied. She was sweating out the admissions, because she'd have to have a scholarship or she couldn't afford to go. Not only that, she'd have to have a job.

She'd worked part-time at a mechanic's shop while her father was alive. He'd drop her off after school and pick her up when she finished work. But his illness had come on quickly and she'd lost the job. Roberta wasn't about to provide transportation.

She rolled over restlessly. Maybe there would be something she could get in San Antonio, perhaps in a convenience store if all else failed. She didn't mind hard work. She was used to it. Since her father had married Roberta, Michelle had done all the cooking and cleaning and laundry. She even mowed the lawn.

Her father had seemed to realize his mistake toward the end. He'd apologized for bringing Roberta into their lives. He'd been lonely since her mother died, and Roberta had flattered him and made him feel good. She'd been fun to be around during the courtship—even Michelle had thought so. Roberta went shopping with the girl, praised her cooking, acted like a really nice person. It wasn't until after the wedding that she'd shown her true colors.

Michelle had always thought it was the alcohol that had made her change so suddenly for the worse. It wasn't discussed in front of her, but Michelle knew that Roberta had been missing for a few weeks, just before her father was diagnosed with cancer. And there was gossip that the doctor had sent his young wife off to a rehabilitation center because of a drinking problem. Afterward, Roberta hadn't been quite so hard to live with. Until they'd moved to Comanche Wells, at least.

Dr. Godfrey had patted Michelle on the shoulder only days before the cancer had taken a sudden turn for the worse and he was bedridden. He'd smiled ruefully.

"I'm very sorry, sweetheart," he'd told her. "If I could go back and change things…"

"I know, Daddy. It's all right."

He'd pulled her close and kissed her forehead. "You're like your mother. She took things to heart, too. You have to learn how to deal with unpleasant people. You have to learn not to take life so seriously.…"

"Alan, are you ever coming inside?" Roberta had interrupted petulantly. She hated seeing her husband and her stepdaughter together. She made every effort to keep them apart. "What are you doing, anyway, looking at those stupid smelly cattle?"

"I'll be there in a moment, Roberta," he called back.

"The dishes haven't been washed," she told Michelle with a cold smile. "Your job, not mine."

She'd gone back inside and slammed the screen. Michelle winced.

So did her father. He drew in a deep breath. "Well, we'll get through this," he said absently. He'd winced again, holding his stomach.

"You should see Dr. Coltrain," she remarked. Dr. Copper Coltrain was one of their local physicians. "You keep putting it off. It's worse, isn't it?"

He sighed. "I guess it is. Okay. I'll see him tomorrow, worrywart."

She grinned. "Okay."

Tomorrow had ended with a battery of tests and a sad prognosis. They'd sent him back home with more medicine and no hope. He'd lasted a few weeks past the diagnosis.

Michelle's eyes filled with tears. The loss was still new, raw. She missed her father. She hated being at the mercy of her stepmother, who wanted nothing more than to sell the house and land right out from under Michelle. In fact, she'd already said that as soon as the will went through probate, she was going to do exactly that.

Michelle had protested. She had several months of school to go. Where would she live?

That, Roberta had said icily, was no concern of hers. She didn't care what happened to her stepdaughter. Roberta was young and had a life of her own, and she wasn't going to spend it smelling cattle and manure. She was going to move in with Bert. He was in between jobs, but the sale of the house and land would keep them for a while. Then they'd go to Las Vegas where she knew people and could make their fortune in the casino.

Michelle had cocked her head and just stared at her

stepmother with a patronizing smile. "Nobody beats the house in Las Vegas," she said in a soft voice.

"I'll beat it," Roberta snapped. "You don't know anything about gambling."

"I know that sane people avoid it," she returned.

Roberta shrugged.

There was only one real-estate agent in Comanche Wells. Michelle called her, nervous and obviously upset.

"Roberta says she's selling the house," she began.

"Relax." Betty Mathers laughed. "She has to get the will through probate, and then she has to list the property. The housing market is in the basement right now, sweetie. She'd have to give it away to sell it."

"Thanks," Michelle said huskily. "You don't know how worried I was…." Her voice broke, and she stopped.

"There's no reason to worry," Betty assured her. "Even if she does leave, you have friends here. Somebody will take the property and make sure you have a place to stay. I'll do it myself if I have to."

Michelle was really crying now. "That's so kind…!"

"Michelle, you've been a fixture around Jacobs County since you were old enough to walk. You spent summers with your grandparents here and you were always doing things to help them, and other people. You spent the night in the hospital with the Harrises' little boy when he had to have that emergency appendectomy and wouldn't let them give you a dime. You baked cakes for the sale that helped Rob Meiner when his house burned. You're always doing for other people. Don't think it doesn't get noticed." Her voice hardened. "And don't think we aren't aware of what your stepmother is up to. She has no friends here, I promise you."

Michelle drew in a breath and wiped her eyes. "She thought Daddy was rich."

"I see," came the reply.

"She hated moving down here. I was never so happy," she added. "I love Comanche Wells."

Betty laughed. "So do I. I moved here from New York City. I like hearing crickets instead of sirens at night."

"Me, too."

"You stop worrying, okay?" she added. "Everything's going to be all right."

"I will. And thanks."

"No thanks necessary."

Michelle was to remember that conversation the very next day. She got home from school that afternoon and her father's prized stamp collection was sitting on the coffee table. A tall, distinguished man was handing Roberta a check.

"It's a marvelous collection," the man said.

"What are you doing?" Michelle exclaimed, dropping her books onto the sofa, as she stared at the man with horror. "You can't sell Daddy's stamps! You can't! It's the only thing of his I have left that we both shared! I helped him put in those stamps, from the time I was in grammar school!"

Roberta looked embarrassed. "Now, Michelle, we've already discussed this...."

"We haven't discussed anything!" she raged, red-faced and weeping. "My father has only been dead three weeks and you've already thrown away every single thing he had, even his clothes! You've talked about selling the house... I'm still in school—I won't even have a place to live. And now this! You...you...mercenary gold digger!"

Roberta tried to smile at the shocked man. "I do apologize for my daughter...."

"I'm not her daughter! She married my father two years ago. She's got a boyfriend. She was with him while my father was dying in the hospital!"

The man stared at Michelle for a long moment, turned to Roberta, snapped the check out of her hands and tore it into shreds.

"But...we had a deal," Roberta stammered.

The man gave her a look that made her move back a step. "Madam, if you were kin to me, I would disown you," he said harshly. "I have no wish to purchase a collection stolen from a child."

"I'll sue you!" Roberta raged.

"By all means. Attempt it."

He turned to Michelle. "I am very sorry," he said gently. "For your loss and for the situation in which you find yourself." He turned to Roberta. "Good day."

He walked out.

Roberta gave him just enough time to get to his car. Then she turned to Michelle and slapped her so hard that her teeth felt as if they'd come loose on that side of her face.

"You little brat!" she yelled. "He was going to give me five thousand dollars for that stamp collection! It took me weeks to find a buyer!"

Michelle just stared at her, cold pride crackling around her. She lifted her chin. "Go ahead. Hit me again. And see what happens."

Roberta drew back her hand. She meant to do it. The child was a horror. She hated her! But she kept remembering the look that minister had given her. She put her hand down and grabbed her purse.

"I'm going to see Bert," she said icily. "And you'll get

no lunch money from me from now on. You can mop floors for your food, for all I care!"

She stormed out the door, got into her car and roared away.

Michelle picked up the precious stamp collection and took it into her room. She had a hiding place that, hopefully, Roberta wouldn't be able to find. There was a loose baseboard in her closet. She pulled it out, slid the stamp book inside and pushed it back into the wall.

She went to the mirror. Her face looked almost blistered where Roberta had hit her. She didn't care. She had the stamp collection. It was a memento of happy times when she'd sat on her father's lap and carefully tucked stamps into place while he taught her about them. If Roberta killed her, she wasn't giving the stamps up.

But she was in a hard place, with no real way out. The months until graduation seemed like years. Roberta would make her life a living hell from now on because she'd opposed her. She was so tired of it. Tired of Roberta. Tired of Bert and his innuendoes. Tired of having to be a slave to her stepmother. It seemed so hopeless.

She thought of her father and started bawling. He was gone. He'd never come back. Roberta would torment her to death. There was nothing left.

She walked out the front door like a sleepwalker, out to the dirt road that lead past the house. And she sat down in the middle of it—heartbroken and dusty with tears running down her cheeks.

Chapter Two

Michelle felt the vibration of the vehicle before she smelled the dust that came up around it. Her back was to the direction it was coming from. Desperation had blinded her to the hope of better days. She was sick of life. Sick of everything.

She put her hands on her knees, brought her elbows in, closed her eyes, and waited for the collision. It would probably hurt. Hopefully, it would be quick....

There was a squealing of tires and a metallic jerk. She didn't feel the impact. Was she dead?

Long, muscular legs in faded blue denim came into view above big black hand-tooled leather boots.

"Would you care to explain what the hell you're doing sitting in the middle of a road?" a deep, angry voice demanded.

She looked up into chilling liquid black eyes and grimaced. "Trying to get hit by a car?"

"I drive a truck," he pointed out.

"Trying to get hit by a truck," she amended in a matter-of-fact tone.

"Care to elaborate?"

She shrugged. "My stepmother will probably beat me when she gets back home because I ruined her sale."

He frowned. "What sale?"

"My father died three weeks ago," she said heavily. She figured he didn't know, because she hadn't seen any signs of life at the house down the road until she'd watched his truck go by just recently. "She had all his things taken to the landfill because I insisted on a real funeral, not a cremation, and now she's trying to sell his stamp collection. It's all I have left of him. I ruined the sale. The man left. She hit me...."

He turned his head. It was the first time he'd noticed the side of her face that looked almost blistered. His eyes narrowed. "Get in the truck."

She stared at him. "I'm all dusty."

"It's a dusty truck. It won't matter."

She got to her feet. "Are you abducting me?"

"Yes."

She sighed. "Okay." She glanced at him ruefully. "If you don't mind, I'd really like to go to Mars. Since I'm being abducted, I mean."

He managed a rough laugh.

She went around to the passenger side. He opened the door for her.

"You're Mr. Brandon," she said when he climbed into the driver's seat and slammed the door.

"Yes."

She drew in a breath. "I'm Michelle."

"Michelle." He chuckled. "There was a song with that

name. My father loved it. One of the lines was 'Michelle, *ma belle*.'" He glanced at her. "Do you speak French?"

"A little," she said. "I have it second period. It means something like 'my beauty.'" She laughed. "And that has nothing to do with me, I'm afraid. I'm just plain."

He glanced at her with raised eyebrows. Was she serious? She was gorgeous. Young, and untried, but her creamy complexion was without a blemish. She was nicely shaped and her hair was a pale blond. Those soft gray eyes reminded him of a fog in August...

He directed his eyes to the road. She was just a child, what was he thinking? "Beauty, as they say, is in the eye of the beholder."

"Do you speak French?" she asked, curious.

He nodded. "French, Spanish, Portuguese, Afrikaans, Norwegian, Russian, German and a handful of Middle Eastern dialects."

"Really?" She was fascinated. "Did you work as a translator or something?"

He pursed his lips. "From time to time," he said, and then laughed to himself.

"Cool."

He started the truck and drove down the road to the house he owned. It wasn't far, just about a half mile. It was a ranch house, set back off the road. There were oceans of flowers blooming around it in the summer, planted by the previous owner, Mrs. Eller, who had died. Of course, it was still just February, and very cold. There were no flowers here now.

"Mrs. Eller loved flowers."

"Excuse me?"

"She lived here all her life," she told him, smiling as they drove up to the front porch. "Her husband worked as a deputy sheriff. They had a son in the military, but he was killed overseas. Her husband died soon afterward. She planted so many flowers that you could never even see the house. I used to come over and visit her when I was little, with my grandfather."

"Your people are from here?"

"Oh, yes. For three generations. Daddy went to medical school in Georgia and then he set up a practice in cardiology in San Antonio. We lived there. But I spent every summer here with my grandparents while they were alive. Daddy kept the place up, after, and it was like a vacation home while Mama was alive." She swallowed. That loss had been harsh. "We still had everything, even the furniture, when Daddy decided to move us down here and take early retirement. She hated it from the first time she saw it." Her face hardened. "She's selling it. My stepmother, I mean. She's already talked about it."

He drew in a breath. He knew he was going to regret this. He got out, opened the passenger door and waited for her to get out. He led the way into the house, seated her in the kitchen and pulled out a pitcher of iced tea. When he had it in glasses, he sat down at the table with her.

"Go ahead," he invited. "Get it off your chest."

"It's not your problem…"

"You involved me in an attempted suicide," he said with a droll look. "That makes it my problem."

She grimaced. "I'm really sorry, Mr. Brandon…."

"Gabriel."

She hesitated.

He raised an eyebrow. "I'm not that old," he pointed out.

She managed a shy smile. "Okay."

He cocked his head. "Say it," he said, and his liquid black eyes stared unblinking into hers.

She felt her heart drop into her shoes. She swallowed

down a hot wave of delight and hoped it didn't show. "Ga...Gabriel," she obliged.

His face seemed to soften. Just a little. He smiled, showing beautiful white teeth. "That's better."

She flushed. "I'm not...comfortable with men," she blurted out.

His eyes narrowed on her face, her averted eyes. "Does your stepmother have a boyfriend?"

She swallowed, hard. The glass in her hand trembled.

He took the glass from her and put it on the table. "Tell me."

It all poured out. Finding Roberta in Bert's arms just after the funeral, finding them on the couch together that day, the way Bert looked and her and tried to touch her, the visit from her minister...

"And I thought my life was complicated," he said heavily. He shook his head. "I'd forgotten what it was like to be young and at the mercy of older people."

She studied him quietly. The expression on his face was...odd.

"You know," she said softly. "You understand."

"I had a stepfather," he said through his teeth. "He was always after my sister. She was very pretty, almost fourteen. I was a few years older, and I was bigger than he was. Our mother loved him, God knew why. We'd moved back to Texas because the international company he worked for promoted him and he had to go to Dallas for the job. One day I heard my sister scream. I went into her room, and there he was. He'd tried to..." He stopped. His face was like stone. "My mother had to get a neighbor to pull me off him. After that, after she knew what had been going on, she still defended him. I was arrested, but the public defender got an earful. He spoke to my sister. My stepfather was arrested, charged, tried. My mother stood by him, the whole time. My sister was victimized by the defense attorney, after what she'd already suffered at our stepfather's hands. She was so traumatized by the experience that she doesn't even date."

She winced. One small hand went shyly to cover his clenched fist on the table. "I'm so sorry."

He seemed to mentally shake himself, as if he'd been locked into the past. He met her soft, concerned gaze. His big hand turned, curled around hers. "I've never spoken of it, until now."

"Maybe sometimes it's good to share problems. Dark memories aren't so bad when you force them into the light."

"Seventeen going on thirty?" he mused, smiling at her. It didn't occur to her to wonder how he knew her age.

She smiled. "There are always people who are in worse shape than you are. My friend Billy has an alcoholic father who beats him and his mother. The police are over there all the time, but his mother will never press charges. Sheriff Carson says the next time, he's going to jail, even if he has to press charges himself."

"Good for the sheriff."

"What happened, after the trial?" she prodded gently.

He curled his fingers around Michelle's, as if he enjoyed their soft comfort. She might have been fascinated to know that he'd never shared these memories with any other woman, and that, as a rule, he hated having people touch him.

"He went to jail for child abuse," he said. "My mother was there every visiting day."

"No, what happened to you and your sister?"

"My mother refused to have us in the house with her. We were going to be placed in foster homes. The public defender had a maiden aunt, childless, who was suicidal. Her problems weren't so terrible, but she tended to depression and she let them take her almost over the edge. So he thought we might be able to help each other. We went to live with Aunt Maude." He chuckled. "She was not what you think of as anybody's maiden aunt. She drove a Jaguar, smoked like a furnace, could drink any grown man under the table, loved bingo parties and cooked like a gourmet. Oh, and she spoke about twenty languages. In her youth, she was in the army and mustered out as a sergeant."

"Wow," she exclaimed. "She must have been fascinating to live with."

"She was. And she was rich. She spoiled us rotten. She got my sister into therapy, for a while at least, and me into the army right after I graduated." He smiled. "She was nuts about Christmas. We had trees that bent at the ceiling, and the limbs groaned under all the decorations. She'd go out and invite every street person she could find over to eat with us." His face sobered. "She said she'd seen foreign countries where the poor were treated better than they were here. Ironically, it was one of the same people she invited to Christmas dinner who stabbed her to death."

She winced. "I'm so sorry!"

"Me, too. By that time, though, Sara and I were grown. I was in the…military," he said, hoping she didn't notice the involuntary pause, "and Sara had her own apartment. Maude left everything she had to the two of us and her nephew. We tried to give our share back to him, as her only blood heir, but he just laughed and said he got to keep his aunt for years longer because of us. He went into private practice and made a fortune defending drug lords, so he didn't really need it, he told us."

"Defending drug lords." She shook her head.

"We all do what we do," he pointed out. "Besides, I've known at least one so-called drug lord who was better than some upright people."

She just laughed.

He studied her small hand. "If things get too rough for you over there, let me know. I'll manage something."

"It's only until graduation this spring," she pointed out.

"In some situations, a few months can be a lifetime," he said quietly.

She nodded.

"Friends help each other."

She studied his face. "Are we? Friends, I mean?"

"We must be. I haven't told anyone else about my stepfather."

"You didn't tell me the rest of it."

His eyes went back to her hand resting in his. "He got out on good behavior six months after his conviction and decided to make my sister pay for testifying against him. She called 911. The police shot him."

"Oh, my gosh."

"My mother blamed both of us for it. She moved back to Canada, to Alberta, where we grew up."

"Are you Canadian?" she asked curiously.

He smiled. "I'm actually Texas born. We moved to Canada to stay with my mother's people when my father was in the military and stationed overseas. Sara was born in Calgary. We lived there until just after my mother married my stepfather."

"Did you see your mother again, after that?" she asked gently.

He shook his head. "Our mother never spoke to us again. She died a few years back. Her attorney tracked me down and said she left her estate, what there was of it, to the cousins in Alberta."

"I'm so sorry."

"Life is what it is. I had hoped she might one day realize what she'd done to my sister. She never did."

"We can't help who we love, or what it does to mess us up."

He frowned. "You really are seventeen going on thirty."

She laughed softly. "Maybe I'm an old soul."

"Ah. Been reading philosophy, have we?"

"Yes." She paused. "You haven't mentioned your father."

He smiled sadly. "He was in a paramilitary group overseas. He stepped on an antipersonnel mine."

She didn't know what a paramilitary group was, so she just nodded.

"He was from Dallas," he continued. "He had a small ranch in Texas that he inherited from his grandfather. He and my mother met at the Calgary Stampede. He trained horses and he'd sold several to be used at the stampede. She had an uncle who owned a ranch in Alberta and also supplied livestock to the stampede." He stared at her small hand in his. "Her people were French-Canadian. One of my grandmothers was a member of the Blackfoot Nation."

"Wow!"

He smiled.

"Then, you're an American citizen," she said.

"Our parents did the whole citizenship process. In short, I now have both Canadian and American citizenship."

"My dad loved this Canadian television show, *Due*

South. He had the whole DVD collection. I liked the Mountie's dog. He was a wolf."

He laughed. "I've got the DVDs, too. I loved the show. It was hilarious."

She glanced at the clock on the wall. "I have to go. If you aren't going to run over me, I'll have to fix supper in case she comes home to eat. It's going to be gruesome. She'll still be furious about the stamp collection." Her face grew hard. "She won't find it. I've got a hiding place she doesn't know about."

He smiled. "Devious."

"Not normally. But she's not selling Daddy's stamps."

He let go of her hand and got up from his chair. "If she hits you again, call 911."

"She'd kill me for that."

"Not likely."

She sighed. "I guess I could, if I had to."

"You mentioned your minister. Who is he?"

"Jake Blair. Why?"

His expression was deliberately blank.

"Do you know him? He's a wonderful minister. Odd thing, my stepmother was intimidated by him."

He hesitated, and seemed to be trying not to laugh. "Yes. I've heard of him."

"He told her that his daughter was going to pick me up and bring me home from church every week. His daughter works for the Jacobsville police chief."

"Cash Grier."

She nodded. "He's very nice."

"Cash Grier?" he exclaimed. "Nice?"

"Oh, I know people talk about him, but he came to speak to my civics class once. He's intelligent."

"Very."

He helped her back into the truck and drove her to her front door.

She hesitated before she got out, turning to him. "Thank you. I don't think I've ever been so depressed. I've never actually tried to kill myself before."

His liquid black eyes searched hers. "We all have days when we're ridden by the 'black dog.'"

She blinked. "Excuse me?"

He chuckled. "Winston Churchill had periods of severe depression. He called it that."

She frowned. "Winston Churchill..."

"There was this really big world war," he said facetiously, with over-the-top enthusiasm, "and this country called England, and it had a leader during—"

"Oh, give me a break!" She burst out laughing.

He grinned at her. "Just checking."

She shook her head. "I know who he was. I just had to put it into context is all. Thanks again."

"Anytime."

She got out and closed the door, noting with relief that Roberta hadn't come home yet. She smiled and waved. He waved back. When he drove off, she noticed that he didn't look back. Not at all.

She had supper ready when Roberta walked in the door. Her stepmother was still fuming.

"I'm not eating beef," she said haughtily. "You know I hate it. And are those mashed potatoes? I'll bet you crammed them with butter!"

"Yes, I did," Michelle replied quietly, "because you always said you liked them that way."

Roberta's cheeks flushed. She shifted, as if the words, in that quiet voice, made her feel guilty.

In fact, they did. She was remembering her behavior

with something close to shame. Her husband had only been dead three weeks. She'd tossed his belongings, refused to go to the funeral, made fun of her stepdaughter at every turn, even slapped her for messing up the sale of stamps which Alan had left to Michelle. And after all that, the child made her favorite food. Her behavior should be raising red flags, but her stepdaughter was, thankfully, too naive to notice it. Bert's doing, she thought bitterly. All his fault.

"You don't have to eat it," Michelle said, turning away.

Roberta made a rough sound in her throat. "It's all right," she managed tautly. She sat down at the table. She glanced at Michelle, who was dipping a tea bag in a cup of steaming water. "Aren't you eating?"

"I had soup."

Roberta made inroads into the meat loaf and mashed potatoes. The girl had even made creamed peas, her favorite.

She started to put her fork down and noticed her hand trembling. She jerked it down onto the wood and pulled her hand back.

It was getting worse. She needed more and more. Bert was complaining about the expense. They'd had a fight. She'd gone storming up to his apartment in San Antonio to cry on his shoulder about her idiot stepdaughter and he'd started complaining when she dipped into his stash. But after all, he was the one who'd gotten her hooked in the first place.

It had taken more money than she'd realized to keep up, and Alan had finally figured out what she was doing. They'd argued. He'd asked her for a divorce, but she'd pleaded with him. She had no place to go. She knew Bert wouldn't hear of her moving in with him. Her whole family was dead.

Alan had agreed, but the price of his agreement was that she had to move down to his hometown with him after he sold his very lucrative practice in San Antonio.

She'd thought he meant the move to be a temporary one. He was tired of the rat race. He wanted something quieter. But they'd only been in his old family homestead for a few days when he confessed that he'd been diagnosed with an inoperable cancer. He wanted to spend some time with his daughter before the end. He wanted to run a free clinic, to help people who had no money for doctors. He wanted his life to end on a positive note, in the place where he was born.

So here was Roberta, stuck after his death with a habit she could no longer afford and no way to break it. Stuck with Cinderella here, who knew about as much about life as she knew about men.

She glared at the girl. She'd really needed the money from those stamps. There was nothing left that she could liquidate for cash. She hadn't taken all of Alan's things to the landfill. She'd told Michelle that so she wouldn't look for them. She'd gone to a consignment shop in San Antonio and sold the works, even his watch. It brought in a few hundred dollars. But she was going through money like water.

"What did you do with the stamps?" Roberta asked suddenly.

Michelle schooled her features to give away nothing, and she turned. "I hitched a ride into town and asked Cash Grier to keep them for me."

Roberta sucked in her breath. Fear radiated from her. "Cash Grier?"

Michelle nodded. "I figured it was the safest place. I told him I was worried about someone stealing them while I was at school."

Which meant she hadn't told the man that Roberta had slapped her. Thank God. All she needed now was an assault charge. She had to be more careful. The girl was too stupid to recognize her symptoms. The police chief wouldn't be. She didn't want anyone from law enforcement on the place. But she didn't even have the grace to blush when Michelle made the comment about someone possibly "stealing" her stamp collection.

She got up from the table. She was thirsty, but she knew it would be disastrous to pick up her cup of coffee. Not until she'd taken what she needed to steady her hands.

She paused on her way to the bathroom, with her back to Michelle. "I'm... I shouldn't have slapped you," she bit off.

She didn't wait for a reply. She was furious with herself for that apology. Why should the kid's feelings matter to her, anyway? She pushed away memories of how welcoming Michelle had been when she first started dating Alan. Michelle had wanted to impress her father's new friend.

Well, that was ancient history now. She was broke and Alan had died, leaving her next to nothing. She picked up her purse from the side table and went into the bathroom with it.

Michelle cleaned off the table and put the dishes into the dishwasher. Roberta hadn't come out of the bathroom even after she'd done all that, so she went to her room.

Michelle had been surprised by the almost-apology. But once she thought about it, she realized that Roberta might think she was going to press charges. She was afraid of her stepmother. She had violent mood swings and she'd threatened to hit Michelle several times.

It was odd, because when she'd first married Dr. Alan Godfrey, Michelle had liked her. She'd been fun to be around. But she had a roving eye. She liked men. If they went to a restaurant, someone always struck up a conversation with Roberta, who was exquisitely groomed and dressed and had excellent manners. Roberta enjoyed masculine attention, without being either coarse or forward.

Then, several months ago, everything had changed. Roberta had started going out at night alone. She told her husband that she'd joined an exercise club at a friend's house, a private one. They did aerobics and Pilates and things like that. Just women.

But soon afterward, Roberta became more careless about her appearance. Her manners slipped, badly. She complained about everything. Alan wasn't giving her enough spending money. The house needed cleaning, why wasn't Michelle doing more when she wasn't in school? She wasn't doing any more cooking, she didn't like it, Michelle would have to take over for her. And on it went. Alan had been devastated by the change. So had Michelle, who had to bear the brunt of most of Roberta's fury.

"Some women have mood swings as they get older," Alan had confided to his daughter, but there was something odd in his tone of voice. "But you mustn't say anything about it to her. She doesn't like thinking she's getting on in years. All right?"

"All right, Daddy," she'd agreed, with a big smile.

He'd hugged her close. "That's my girl."

Roberta had gone away for a few weeks after that. Then, not too long after her return, they'd moved to Comanche Wells, into the house where Michelle had spent so many happy weeks with her grandparents every summer.

The elderly couple had died in a wreck only a few years after Michelle's mother had died of a stroke. It had been a blow. Her father had gone through terrible grief. But then, so had Michelle.

Despite the double tragedy, Comanche Wells and this house seemed far more like home than San Antonio ever had, because it was so small that Michelle knew almost every family who lived in it. She knew people in Jacobsville, too, of course, but it was much larger. Comanche Wells was tiny by comparison.

Michelle loved the farm animals that her grandparents had kept. They always had dogs and cats and chickens for her to play with. But by the time Alan moved his family down here, there was only the small herd of beef cattle. Now the herd had been sold and was going to a local rancher who was going to truck the steers over to his own ranch.

Her door opened suddenly. Roberta looked wild-eyed. "I'm going back up to San Antonio for the night. I have to see Bert."

"All…" She had started to say "all right," but the door slammed. Roberta went straight out to her car, revved it up and scattered gravel on the way to the road.

It was odd behavior, even for her.

Michelle felt a little better than she had. At least she and Roberta might be able to manage each other's company until May, when graduation rolled around.

But Gabriel had helped her cope with what she thought was unbearable. She smiled, remembering his kindness, remembering the strong, warm clasp of his fingers. Her heart sailed at the memory. She'd almost never held hands with a boy. Once, when she was twelve, at a school dance. But the boy had moved away, and she was far too shy and old-fashioned to appeal to most of the boys in her high school classes. There had been another boy, at high school, but that date had ended in near disaster.

Gabriel was no boy. He had to be at least in his mid-twenties. He would think of her as a child. She grimaced. Well, she was growing up. One day...who knew what might happen?

She opened her English textbook and got busy with her homework. Then she remembered with a start what she'd told Roberta, that lie about having Cash Grier keep the stamp book. What if Roberta asked him?

Her face flamed. It would be a disaster. She'd lied, and Roberta would know it. She'd tear the house apart looking for that collection...

Then Michelle calmed down. Roberta seemed afraid of Cash Grier. Most people were. She doubted very seriously that her stepmother would approach him. But just to cover her bases, she was going to stop by his office after school. She could do it by pretending to ask Carlie what time she would pick her up for church services. Then maybe she could work up the nerve to tell him what she'd done. She would go without lunch. That would give her just enough money to pay for a cab home from Jacobsville, which was only a few miles away. Good thing she already had her lunch money for the week, because Roberta had told her there wouldn't be any more. She was going to have to do without lunch from now on, apparently. Or get a job. And good luck to that, without a car or a driver's license.

She sighed. Her life was more complicated than it had ever been. But things might get better. Someday.

Chapter Three

Michelle got off the school bus in downtown Jacobsville on Friday afternoon. She had to stop by the newspaper office to ask Minette Carson if she'd give her a reference for the scholarship she was applying for. The office was very close to police chief Grier's office, whom she also needed to see. And she had just enough money to get the local cab company to take her home.

Minette was sitting out front at her desk when Michelle walked in. She grinned and got up to greet her.

"How's school?" she asked.

"Going very well," Michelle said. "I wanted to ask if I could put you down as a reference. I'm applying for that journalism scholarship we spoke about last month, at Marist College in San Antonio."

"Of course you can."

"Thanks. I'm hoping I can keep my grades up so I'll have a shot at it."

"You'll do fine, Michelle. You have a way with words." She held up a hand when Michelle looked as if she might protest. "I never lie about writing. I'm brutally honest. If I thought you didn't have the skill, I'd keep my mouth shut."

Michelle laughed. "Okay. Thanks, then."

Minette perched on the edge of her desk. "I was wondering if you might like to work part-time for me. After school and Saturday morning."

Michelle's jaw dropped. "You mean, work here?" she exclaimed. "Oh, my gosh, I'd love to!" Then the joy drained out of her face. "I can't," she groaned. "I don't drive, and I don't have cab fare home. I mean, I do today, but I went without lunch...." Her face flamed.

"Carlie lives just past you," she said gently. "She works until five. So do we. I know she'd let you ride with her. She works Saturday mornings, too."

The joy came back into her features. "I'll ask her!"

Minette chuckled. "Do that. And let me know."

"I will, I promise."

"You can start Monday, if you like. Do you have a cell phone?" Minette asked.

Michelle hesitated and shook her head with lowered eyes.

"Don't worry about it. We'll get you one."

"Oh, but...."

"I'll have you phoning around town for news. Junior reporter stuff," she added with a grin. "A cell's an absolute necessity."

"In that case, okay, but I'll pay you back."

"That's a deal."

"I'll go over and talk to Carlie."

"Stop back by and let me know, okay?"

"Okay!"

She didn't normally rush, but she was so excited that her feet carried her across the street like wings.

She walked into the police station. Cash Grier was perched on Carlie's desk, dictating from a paper he held in his hand. He stopped when he saw Michelle.

"Sorry," Michelle said, coloring. She clutched her textbooks to her chest almost as a shield. "I just needed to ask Carlie something. I can come back later...."

"Nonsense," Cash said, and grinned.

She managed a shy smile. "Thanks." She hesitated. "I told a lie to my stepmother," she blurted out. "I think you should know, because it involved you."

His dark eyebrows arched. "Really? Did you volunteer me for the lead in a motion picture or something? Because I have to tell you, my asking price is extremely high...."

She laughed with pure delight. "No. I told her I gave you my father's stamp collection for safekeeping." She flushed again. "She was going to sell it. She'd already thrown away all his stuff. He and I worked on the stamp collection together as long as I can remember. It's all I have left of him." She swallowed. Hard.

Cash got up. He towered over her. He wasn't laughing. "You bring it in here and I'll put it in the safe," he said gently. "Nobody will touch it."

"Thanks." She was trying not to cry. "That's so kind..."

"Now, don't cry or you'll have me in tears. What would people think? I mean, I'm a big, tough cop. I can't be seen standing around sobbing all over the place. Crime would flourish!"

That amused her. She stopped biting her lip and actually grinned.

"That's better." His black eyes narrowed quizzically.

"Your stepmother seems to have some issues. I got an earful from your minister this morning."

She nodded sadly. "She was so different when we lived in San Antonio. I mean, we went shopping together, we took turns cooking. Then we moved down here and she got mixed up with that Bert person." She shivered. "He gives me cold chills, but she's crazy about him."

"Bert Sims?" Cash asked in a deceptively soft tone.

"That's him."

Cash didn't say anything else. "If things get rough over there, call me, will you? I know you're outside the city limits, but I can get to Hayes Carson pretty quick if I have to, and he has jurisdiction."

"Oh, it's nothing like that...."

"Isn't it?" Cash asked.

She felt chilled. It was as if he was able to see Roberta through her eyes, and he saw everything.

"She did apologize. Sort of. For hitting me, I mean."

"Hitting you?" Cash stood straighter. "When?"

"I messed up the sale of Daddy's stamps. She was wild-eyed and screaming. She just slapped me, is all. She's been excitable since before Daddy died, but now she's just...just...nuts. She talks about money all the time, like she's dying to get her hands on some. But she doesn't buy clothes or cosmetics, she doesn't even dress well anymore."

"Do you know why?"

She shook her head. She drew in a breath. "She doesn't drink," she said. "I know that's what you're thinking. She and Daddy used to have drinks every night, and she had a problem for a little while, but she got over it."

Cash just nodded. "You let me know if things get worse. Okay?"

"Okay, Chief. Thanks," she added.

The phone rang. Carlie answered it. "It's your wife," she said with a big grin.

Cash's face lit up. "Really? Wow. A big-time movie star calling me up on the phone. I'm just awed, I am." He grinned. Everybody knew his wife, Tippy, had been known as the Georgia Firefly when she'd been a supermodel and, later, an actress. "I'll take it in my office. With the door closed." He made a mock scowl. "And no eavesdropping."

Carlie put her hand over her heart. "I swear."

"Not in my office, you don't," he informed her. "Swearing is a misdemeanor."

She stuck out her tongue at his departing back.

"I saw that," he said without looking behind him. He went into his office and closed the door on two giggling women.

"He's a trip to work for," Carlie enthused, her green eyes sparkling in a face framed by short, dark, wavy hair. "I was scared to death of him when I interviewed for the job. At least, until he accused me of hiding his bullets and telling his men that he read fashion magazines in the bathroom."

Michelle laughed.

"He's really funny. He says he keeps files on aliens in the filing cabinet and locks it so I won't peek." The smile moderated. "But if there's an emergency, he's the toughest guy I've ever known. I would never cross him, if I was a criminal."

"They say he chased a speeder all the way to San Antonio once."

She laughed. "That wasn't the chief. That was Kilraven, who worked here undercover." She leaned forward. "He really belongs to a federal agency. We're not supposed to mention it."

"I won't tell," Michelle promised.

"However, the chief—" she nodded toward his closed door "—got on a plane to an unnamed foreign country, tossed a runaway criminal into a bag and boated him to Miami. The criminal was part of a drug cartel. He killed a small-town deputy because he thought the man was a spy. He wasn't, but he was just as dead. Then the feds got involved and the little weasel escaped into a country that didn't have an extradition treaty with us. However, once he was on American soil, he was immediately arrested by Dade County deputies." She grinned. "The chief denied ever having seen the man, and nobody could prove that it was him on the beach. And," she added darkly, "you never heard that from me. Right?"

"Right!"

Carlie laughed. "So what can I do for you?"

"I need a ride home from work."

"I've got another hour to go, but…"

"Not today," Michelle said. "Starting Monday. Minette Carson just offered me a part-time job, but I don't have a way to get home. And she said I could work part-time Saturday, but I can't drive and I don't have a car."

"You can ride with me, and I'd welcome the company," Carlie said easily.

"I'll chip in for the gas."

"That would really help! Have you seen what I drive?" She groaned. "My dad has this thing about cars. He thinks you need an old truck to keep you from speeding, so he bought me a twelve-year-old tank. At least, it looks like a tank." She frowned. "Maybe it was a tank and he had it remodeled. Anyway, it barely gets twelve miles to a gallon and it won't go over fifty." She shook her head. "He drives a vintage Ford Cobra," she added with a scowl. "One of the neatest rides on the planet and I'm not allowed to touch it, can you believe that?"

Michelle just grinned. She didn't know anything about cars. She did recall the way the minister had peeled out of the driveway, scattering gravel. That car he drove had one big engine.

"Your dad scared my stepmother." Michelle laughed. "She wasn't letting me go to church. Your dad said I could ride with you." She stopped and flushed. "I really feel like I'm imposing. I wish I could drive. I wish I had a car...."

"It's really not imposing," Carlie said softly, smiling. "As I said, I'd like the company. I go down lots of back roads getting here from Comanche Wells. I'm not spooky or anything, but this guy did try to kill my Dad with a knife." She lowered her eyes. "I got in the way."

Michelle felt guilty that she hadn't remembered. "I'll learn karate," she promised. "We can go to a class together or something, and if anybody attacks us we can fight back!"

"Bad idea," Cash said, rejoining them. "A few weeks of martial arts won't make you an expert. Even an expert," he added solemnly, "knows better than to fight if he can get away from an armed man."

"That isn't what the ads say," Carlie mused, grinning.

"Yes, I know," Cash replied. "Take it from me, disarming someone with a gun is difficult even for a black belt." He leaned forward. "Which I am."

Carlie stood up, bowed deeply from the waist, and said, "Sensei!" Cash lost it. He roared with laughter.

"You could teach us," Michelle suggested. "Couldn't you?"

Cash just smiled. "I suppose it wouldn't hurt. Just a few basics for an emergency. But if you have an armed opponent, you run," he said firmly. "Or if you're cornered, scream, make a fuss. Never," he emphasized, "get into a car with anyone who threatens to kill you if you don't. Once he's got you in a car, away from help, you're dead, anyway."

Michelle felt chills run down her spine. "Okay."

Carlie looked uncomfortable. She knew firsthand about an armed attacker. Unconsciously, she rubbed the shoulder where the knife had gone in. She'd tried to protect her father. Her assailant had been arrested, but had died soon afterward. She never knew why her father had been the target of an attack by a madman.

"Deep thoughts?" Michelle asked her.

She snapped back. "Sorry. I was remembering the guy who attacked my father." She frowned. "What sort of person attacks a minister, for goodness' sake!"

"Come on down to federal lockup with me, and I'll show you a baker's dozen who have," Cash told her. "Religious arguments quite often lead to murder, even in families. That's why," he added, "we don't discuss politics or religion in the office." He frowned. "Well, if someone died in here, we'd probably say a prayer. And if the president came to see me, and why wouldn't he, we'd probably discuss his foreign policy."

"Why would the president come to see you?" Michelle asked innocently.

Cash pursed his lips. "For advice, of course. I have some great ideas about foreign policy."

"For instance?" Carlie mused.

"I think we should declare war on Tahiti."

They both stared at him.

"Well, if we do, we can send troops, right?" he continued. "And what soldier in his right mind wouldn't want to go and fight in Tahiti? Lush tropical flowers, fire-dancing, beautiful women, the ocean..."

"Tahiti doesn't have a standing army, I don't think," Michelle ventured.

"All the better. We can just occupy it for like three weeks, let them surrender, and then give them foreign aid." He glowered. "Now you've done it. You'll repeat that everywhere and the president will hear about it and he'll never have to come and hear me explain it. You've blown my chances for an invitation to the White House," he groaned. "And I did so want to spend a night in the Lincoln bedroom!"

"Listen, break out those files on aliens that you keep in your filing cabinet and tell the president you've got them!" Carlie suggested, while Michelle giggled. "He'll come right down here to have a look at them!"

"They won't let him," Cash sighed. "His security clearance isn't high enough."

"What?" Carlie exclaimed.

"Well, he's only in the office for four years, eight tops. So the guys in charge of the letter agencies—the really secretive ones—allegedly keep some secrets to themselves. Particularly those dealing with aliens." He chuckled.

The girls, who didn't know whether to believe him or not, just laughed along with him.

Michelle stopped back by Minette's office to tell her the good news, and to thank her again for the job.

"You know," she said, "Chief Grier is really nice."

"Nice when he likes you," Minette said drily. "There are a few criminals in maximum-security prisons who might disagree."

"No doubt there."

"So, will Monday suit you, to start to work?" Minette asked.

"I'd really love to start yesterday." Michelle laughed. "I'm so excited!"

Minette grinned. "Monday will come soon enough. We'll see you then."

"Can you write me a note? Just in case I need one?" She was thinking of how to break it to Roberta. That was going to be tricky.

"No problem." Minette went to her desk, typed out an explanation of Michelle's new position, and signed it. She handed it to the younger woman. "There you go."

"Dress code?" Michelle asked, glancing around the big open room where several people were sitting at desks, to a glass-walled room beyond which big sheets of paper rested on a long section like a chalkboard.

"Just be neat," Minette said easily. "I mostly kick around in jeans and T-shirts, although I dress when I go to political meetings or to interviews with state or federal politicians. You'll need to learn how to use a camera, as well. We have digital ones. They're very user-friendly."

"This is very exciting," Michelle said, her gray eyes glimmering with delight.

Minette laughed. "It is to me, too, and I've done this since I was younger than you are. I grew up running around this office." She looked around with pure love in her eyes. "It's home."

"I'm really looking forward to it. Will I just be reporting news?"

"No. Well, not immediately, at least. You'll learn every aspect of the business, from selling ads to typing copy to composition. Even subscriptions." She leaned forward. "You'll learn that some subscribers probably used to be doctors, because the handwriting looks more like Sanskrit than English."

Michelle chuckled. "I'll cope. My dad had the worst handwriting in the world."

"And he was a doctor," Minette agreed, smiling.

The smile faded. "He was a very good doctor," she said, trying not to choke up. "Sorry," she said, wiping away a tear. "It's still hard."

"It takes time," Minette said with genuine sympathy. "I lost my mother, my stepfather, my stepmother—I loved them all. You'll adjust, but you have to get through the grief process first. Tears are healing."

"Thanks."

"If you need to talk, I'm here. Anytime. Night or day."

Michelle wiped away more tears. "That's really nice of you."

"I know how it feels."

The phone rang and one of the employees called out. "For you, boss. The mayor returning your call."

Minette grimaced. "I have to take it. I'm working on a story about the new water system. It's going to be super."

"I'll see you after school Monday, then. And thanks again."

"My pleasure."

Michelle went home with dreams of journalism dancing in her head. She'd never been so happy. Things were really looking up.

She noted that Roberta's car was in the driveway and she mentally braced herself for a fight. It was suppertime and she hadn't been there to cook. She was going to be in big trouble.

Sure enough, the minute she walked in the door, Roberta threw her hands up and glared at her. "I'm not cooking," she said furiously. "That's your job. Where the hell have you been?"

Michelle swallowed. "I was in…in town."

"Doing what?" came the tart query.

She shifted. "Getting a job."

"A job?" She frowned, and her eyes didn't seem to quite focus. "Well, I'm not driving you to work, even if somebody was crazy enough to hire you!"

"I have a ride," she replied.

"A job," she scoffed. "As if you're ever around to do chores as it is. You're going to get a job? Who's going to do the laundry and the housecleaning and the cooking?"

Michelle bit her tongue, trying not to say what she was thinking. "I have to have money for lunch," she said, thinking fast.

Roberta blinked, then she remembered that she'd said Michelle wasn't getting any more lunch money. She averted her eyes.

"Besides, I have to save for college. I'll start in the fall semester."

"Jobs. College." Roberta looked absolutely furious. "And you think I'm going to stay down here in this hick town while you sashay off to college in some big city, do you?"

"I graduate in just over three months…"

"I'm putting the house on the market," Roberta shot back. She held up a hand. "Don't even bother arguing. I'm listing the house with a San Antonio broker, not one from here." She gave Michelle a dirty look. "They're all on your side, trying to keep the property off the market. It won't work. I need money!"

For just one instant, Michelle thought about letting her have the stamps. Then she decided it was useless to do that. Roberta would spend the money and still try to sell the house. She comforted herself with what the local Realtor had told her—that it would take time for the will to get through probate. If there was a guardian angel, perhaps hers would drag out the time required for all that. And even then, there was a chance the house wouldn't sell.

"I don't imagine a lot of people want to move to a town this small," Michelle said out loud.

"Somebody local might buy it. One of those ranchers." She made it sound like a dirty word.

That made Michelle feel better. If someone from here bought the house, they might consider renting it to her. Since she had a job, thanks to Minette, she could probably afford reasonable rent.

Roberta wiped her face. She was sweating.

Michelle frowned. "Are you all right?"

"Of course I'm all right, I'm just hungry!"

"I'll make supper." She went to her room to put her books away and stopped short. The place was in shambles. Drawers had been emptied, the clothes from the shelves in the closet were tossed haphazardly all over the floor. Michelle's heart jumped, but she noticed without looking too hard that the baseboards in the closet were still where they should be. She looked around but not too closely. After all, she'd told Roberta that Chief Grier had her father's stamp collection. It hadn't stopped Roberta from searching the room. But it was obvious that she hadn't found anything.

She went back out into the hall, where her stepmother was standing with folded arms, a disappointed look on her face. She'd expected that the girl would go immediately to where she'd hidden the stamps. The fact that she didn't even search meant they weren't here. Damn the luck, she really had taken them to the police chief. And even Roberta wasn't brash enough to walk up to Cash Grier and demand the stamp collection back, although she was probably within her legal rights to do so.

"Don't tell me," Michelle said, staring at her. "Squirrels?"

Roberta was disconcerted. Without meaning to, she burst out laughing at the girl's audacity. She turned away, shaking her head. "All right, I just wanted to make sure the stamp collection wasn't still here. I guess you were telling the truth all along."

"Roberta, if you need money so much, why don't you get a job?"

"I had a job, if you recall," she replied. "I worked in retail."

That was true. Roberta had worked at the cosmetics counter in one of San Antonio's most prestigious department stores.

"But I'm not going back to that," Roberta scoffed. "Once I sell this dump of a house, I'll be able to go to New York or Los Angeles and find a man who really is rich, instead of one who's just pretending to be," she added sarcastically.

"Gosh. Poor Bert," Michelle said. "Does he know?"

Roberta's eyes flashed angrily. "If you say a word to him...!"

Michelle held up both hands. "Not my business."

"Exactly!" Roberta snapped. "Now, how about fixing supper?"

"Sure," Michelle agreed. "As soon as I clean up my room," she added in a bland tone.

Her stepmother actually flushed. She took a quick breath. She was shivering. "I need...more..." she mumbled to herself. She went back into her own room and slammed the door.

They ate together, but Michelle didn't taste much of her supper. Roberta read a fashion magazine while she spooned food into her mouth.

"Where are you getting a job? Who's going to even hire a kid like you?" she asked suddenly.

"Minette Carson."

The magazine stilled in her hands. "You're going to work for a newspaper?"

"Of course. I want to study journalism in college."

Roberta looked threatened. "Well, I don't want you working for newspapers. Find something else."

"I won't," Michelle said firmly. "This is what I want to do for a living. I have to start somewhere. And I have to save for college. Unless you'd like to volunteer to pay my tuition…."

"Ha! Fat chance!" Roberta scoffed.

"That's what I thought. I'm going to a public college, but I still have to pay for books and tuition."

"Newspapers. Filthy rags." Her voice sounded slurred. She was picking at her food. Her fork was moving in slow motion. And she was still sweating.

"They do a great deal of good," Michelle argued. "They're the eyes and ears of the public."

"Nosy people sticking their heads into things that don't concern them!"

Michelle looked down at her plate. She didn't mention that people without things to hide shouldn't have a problem with that.

Roberta took her paper towel and mopped her sweaty face. She seemed disoriented and she was flushed, as well.

"You should see a doctor," Michelle said quietly. "There's that flu still going around."

"I'm not sick," the older woman said sharply. "And my health is none of your business!"

Michelle grimaced. She sipped milk instead of answering.

"It's too hot in here. You don't have to keep the thermostat so high!"

"It's seventy degrees," Michelle said, surprised. "I can't keep it higher or we couldn't afford the gas bill." She paid the bills with money that was grudgingly supplied by Roberta from the joint bank account she'd had with Michelle's father. Roberta hadn't lifted a finger to pay a bill since Alan had died.

"Well, it's still hot!" came the agitated reply. She got up from the table. "I'm going outside. I can't breathe in here."

Michelle watched her go with open curiosity. Odd. Roberta seemed out of breath and flushed more and more lately. She had episodes of shaking that seemed very unusual. She acted drunk sometimes, but Michelle knew she wasn't drinking. There was no liquor in the house. It probably was the flu. She couldn't understand why a person who was obviously sick wouldn't just go to the doctor in the first—

There was a loud thud from the general direction of the front porch.

Chapter Four

Michelle got up from her chair and went out onto the porch. It sounded as if Roberta had flung a chair against the wall, maybe in another outburst of temper.

She opened the door and stopped. Roberta was lying there, on her back on the porch, gasping for breath, her eyes wide, her face horrified.

"It's all right, I'll call 911!" She ran for the phone and took it outside with her while she pushed in the emergency services number.

Roberta was grimacing. "The pain!" she groaned. "Hurts…so…bad! Michelle…!"

Roberta held out her hand. Michelle took it, held it, squeezed it comfortingly.

"Jacobs County 911 Center," came a gentle voice on the line. "Is this an emergency?"

"Yes. This is Michelle Godfrey. My stepmother is complaining of chest pain. She's short of breath and barely conscious."

"We'll get someone right out there. Stay on the line."

"Yes, of course."

"Help me," Roberta sobbed.

Michelle's hand closed tighter around her stepmother's. "The EMTs are on the way," she said gently. "It will be all right."

"Bert," Roberta choked. "Damn Bert! It's…his… fault!"

"Please don't try to get up," Michelle said, holding the older woman down. "Lie still."

"I'll…kill him," Roberta choked. "I'll kill him…!"

"Roberta, lie still," Michelle said firmly.

"Oh, God, it hurts!" Roberta sobbed. "My chest…. my chest…!"

Sirens were becoming noticeable in the distance.

"They're almost there, dear," the operator said gently. "Just a few more minutes."

"Yes, I hear them," Michelle said. "She says her chest hurts."

There was muffled conversation in the background, on the phone.

Around the curve, the ambulance shot toward her leaving a wash of dust behind it. Roberta's grip on Michelle's hand was painful.

The older woman was white as a sheet. The hand Michelle was holding was cold and clammy. "I'm…sorry," Roberta bit off. Tears welled in her eyes. "He said it wasn't…pure! He swore…! It was too…much…" She gasped for breath. "Don't let Bert…get away…with it…" Her eyes closed. She shivered. The hand holding Michelle's went slack.

The ambulance was in the driveway now, and a man and a woman jumped out of it and ran toward the porch.

"She said her chest hurt." Michelle faltered as she got

out of the way. "And she couldn't breathe." Tears were salty in her eyes.

Roberta had never been really kind to her, except at the beginning of her relationship with Michelle's father. But the woman was in such pain. It hurt her to see anyone like that, even a mean person.

"Is she going to be all right?" Michelle asked.

They ignored her. They were doing CPR. She recognized it, because one of the Red Cross people had come to her school and demonstrated it. In between compressions one EMT ran to the truck and came back with paddles. They set the machine up and tried to restart Roberta's heart. Once. Twice. Three times. In between there were compressions of the chest and hurried communications between the EMTs and a doctor at the hospital.

After a few minutes, one EMT looked at the other and shook his head. They stood up. The man turned to Michelle. "I'm very sorry."

"Sorry. Sorry?" She looked down at the pale, motionless woman on the dusty front porch with a blank expression. "You mean, she's…?"

They nodded. "We'll call the coroner and have him come out, and we'll notify the sheriff's department, since you're outside the city limits. We can't move her until he's finished. Do you want to call the funeral home and make arrangements?"

"Yes, uh, yes." She pushed her hair back. She couldn't believe this. Roberta was dead? How could she be dead? She just stood there, numb, while the EMTs loaded up their equipment and went back out to the truck.

"Is there someone who can stay with you until the coroner gets here?" the female EMT asked softly, staring worriedly at Michelle.

She stared back at the woman, devoid of thought. Roberta was dead. She'd watched her die. She was in shock.

Just as the reality of the situation really started to hit her, a pickup truck pulled up into the driveway, past the EMT vehicle, and stopped. A tall, good-looking man got out of it, paused to speak to the male EMT and then came right up to the porch.

Without a word, he pulled Michelle into his arms and held her, rocked her. She burst into tears.

"I'll take care of her," he told the female EMT with a smile.

"Thanks," she said. "She'll need to make arrangements...."

"I'll handle it."

"We've notified the authorities," the EMT added. "The sheriff's department and the coroner should arrive shortly." The EMTs left, the ambulance silent and grim now, instead of alive with light and sound, as when it had arrived.

Michelle drank in the scent that clung to Gabriel, the smells of soap and spicy cologne, the leather smell of his jacket. Beneath that, the masculine odor of his skin. She pressed close into his arms and let the tears fall.

Zack Tallman arrived just behind the coroner. Michelle noted the activity on the front porch, but she didn't want to see Roberta's body again. She didn't go outside.

She heard Gabriel and the lawman and the coroner discussing things, and there was the whirring sound a camera made. She imagined that they were photographing Roberta. She shivered. It was so sudden. They'd just had supper and Roberta went outside because she was hot. And then Roberta was dead. It didn't seem real, somehow.

A few minutes later, she heard the coroner's van drive away. Gabriel and Zack Tallman came in together. Zack was handsome, tall, lean and good-looking. His eyes were almost as dark as Gabriel's, but he looked older than Gabriel did.

"The coroner thinks it was a heart attack," Zack was saying. "They'll have to do an autopsy, however. It's required in cases of sudden death."

"Hayes told me that Yancy Dean went back to Florida," Gabriel said. "He was the only investigator you had, wasn't he?"

"He was," Zack said, "so when he resigned, I begged Hayes on my knees for the investigator's position. It's a peach of a job."

"Pays about the same as a senior deputy," Gabriel mused, tongue in cheek.

"Yes, but I get to go to seminars and talk to forensic anthropologists and entomologists and do hard-core investigative work," he added. He chuckled. "I've been after Yancy's job forever. Not that he was bad at it—he was great. But his parents needed him in Florida and he was offered his old job back with Dade County SO," he added, referring to the sheriff's office.

"Well, it worked out for both of you, then," Gabriel said.

"Yes." He sobered as Michelle came into the living room from the kitchen. "Michelle, I'm sorry about your stepmother. I know it must be hard, coming so close on the heels of your father passing."

"Thanks, Mr. Tallman," she replied gently. "Yes, it is." She shook her head. "I still have to talk to the funeral director."

"I'll take care of that for you," Gabriel told her.

"Thanks," she added.

"Michelle, can you tell me how it happened?" Zack asked her.

"Of course." She went through the afternoon, ending with Roberta feeling too hot and going out on the porch to cool off.

He stopped her when she mentioned what Roberta had said about Bert and had her repeat Roberta's last words. He frowned. "I'd like to see her room."

Michelle led the way. The room was a mess. Roberta never picked anything up, and Michelle hadn't had time to do any cleaning. She was embarrassed at the way it looked. But Zack wasn't interested in the clutter. He started going through drawers until he opened the one in the bedside table.

He pulled out his digital camera and shot several photos of the drawer and its contents before he put on a pair of gloves, reached into it and pulled out an oblong case. He dusted the case for fingerprints before he opened it on the table and photographed that, too, along with a small vial of white powder. He turned to Gabriel who exchanged a long look with him.

"That explains a lot," Zack said. "I'll take this up to the crime lab in San Antonio and have them run it for us, but I'm pretty sure what it is and where she got it."

"What is it?" Michelle asked, curious.

"Something evil," Zack said.

Michelle wasn't dense. "Drugs," she said icily. "It's drugs, isn't it?"

"Hard narcotics," Zack agreed.

"That's why she was so crazy all the time," Michelle said heavily. "She drank to excess when we lived in San Antonio. Dad got her into treatment and made her quit. I was sure she was okay, because we didn't have any liquor here. But she had these awful mood swings, and sometimes she hit me…" She bit her lip.

"Well, people under the influence aren't easy to live with," Zack replied heavily. "Not at all."

Zack sat down with Michelle and Gabriel at the kitchen table and questioned Michelle further about Roberta's recent routine, including trips to see Bert Sims in San Antonio. Roberta's last words were telling. He wrote it all down and gave Michelle a form to fill out with all the pertinent information about the past few hours. When she finished, he took it with him.

There was no real crime scene, since Roberta died of what was basically a heart attack brought on by a drug overdose. The coroner's assistant took photos on the front porch, adding to Zack's, so there was a record of where Roberta died. But the house wasn't searched, beyond Zack's thorough documentation of Roberta's room.

"Bert Sims may try to come around to see if Roberta had anything left, to remove evidence," Zack said solemnly to Michelle. "It isn't safe for you to be here alone."

"I've got that covered," Gabriel said with a smile. "Nobody's going to touch her."

Zack smiled. "I already had that figured out," he mused, and Gabriel cleared his throat.

"I have a chaperone in mind," Gabriel replied. "Just so you know."

Zack patted him on the back. "I figured that out already, too." He nodded toward Michelle. "Sorry again."

"Me, too," Michelle said sadly.

Michelle made coffee while Gabriel spoke to his sister, Sara, on the phone. She couldn't understand what he was saying. He was speaking French. She recognized it, but it was a lot more complicated than, "My brother has a brown suit," which was about her level of skill in the language.

His voice was low, and urgent. He spoke again, listened, and then spoke once more. *"C'est bien,"* he concluded, and hung up.

"That was French," Michelle said.

"Yes." He sat down at the table and toyed with the thick white mug she'd put in front of him. There was good china, too—Roberta had insisted on it when she and Alan first married. But the mug seemed much more Gabriel's style than fancy china. She'd put a mug at her place, as well. She had to have coffee in the morning or she couldn't even get to school.

"This morning everything seemed much less complicated," she said after she'd poured coffee. He refused cream and sugar, and she smiled. She didn't take them, either.

"You think you're going in a straight line, and life puts a curve in the way," he agreed with a faint smile. "I know you didn't get along with her. But she was part of your family. It must sting a bit."

"It does," she agreed, surprised at his perception. "She was nice to me when she and Daddy were dating," she added. "Taught me how to cook new things, went shopping with me, taught me about makeup and stuff." She grimaced. "Not that I ever wear it. I hate the way powder feels on my face, and I don't like gunking up my eyes and mouth with pasty cosmetics." She looked at him and saw an odd expression on his face. "That must sound strange...."

He laughed and sipped coffee before he spoke. "Actually, I was thinking how sane it sounded." He quietly studied her for a couple of moments. "You don't need makeup. You're quite pretty enough without it."

She gaped at him.

"Michelle, *ma belle,*" he said in an odd, soft, deep tone, and he smiled.

She went scarlet. She knew her heart was shaking her to death, that he could see it, and she didn't care. He was simply the most gorgeous man she'd ever seen, and he thought she was pretty. A stupid smile turned her lips up, elongating the perfect bow shape they made.

"Sorry," he said gently. "I was thinking out loud, not hitting on you. This is hardly the time."

"Would you like to schedule a time?" she asked with wide, curious eyes. "Because my education in that department is really sad. This one boy tried to kiss me and missed and almost broke my nose. After that, I didn't get another date until the junior prom." She leaned forward. "He was gay and so sweet and shy about it…well, he asked me and told me the reason very honestly. And I said I'd go with him to the prom because of the way my other date had ended. I mean, he wasn't likely to try to kiss me and break my nose and all… Why are you laughing?"

"Marshmallow," he accused, and his smile was full of affectionate amusement.

"Well, yes, I guess I am. But he's such a nice boy. Several of us know about him, but there are these two guys on the football squad that he's afraid of. They're always making nasty remarks to him. He thought if he went with a girl to a dance, they might back off."

"Did they?" he asked, curious.

"Yes, but not because he went with me," she said. She glowered at the memory. "One of them made a nasty remark to him when we were dancing, next to the refreshment table, and I filled a big glass with punch and threw it in his face." She grinned. "I got in big trouble until the gym coach was told why I did it. His brother's gay." The grin got bigger. "He said next time I should use the whole pitcher."

He burst out laughing. "Well, your attitude toward modern issues is…unique. This is a very small town," he explained when her eyebrows went up.

"Oh, I see. You think we treat anybody different like a fungus." She nodded.

"Not exactly. But we hear things about small towns," he began.

"No bigots here. Well, except for Chief Grier."

He blinked. "Your police chief is a bigot?"

She nodded. "He is severely prejudiced against people from other planets. You should just hear him talk about how aliens are going to invade us one day to get their hands on our cows. He thinks they have a milk addiction, and that's why you hear about cattle mutilations… You're laughing again."

He wiped his eyes. She couldn't know that he rarely laughed. His life had been a series of tragedies. Humor had never been part of it. She made him feel light inside, almost happy.

"I can see the chief's point," he managed.

"Cow bigot," she accused, and he almost fell on the floor.

She wrapped her cold hands around her mug. "I guess I shouldn't be cracking jokes, with Roberta dead…" Her eyes burned with tears. "I still can't believe it. Roberta's gone. She's gone." She drew in a breath and sipped coffee. "We've done nothing but argue since Daddy died. But she wanted me to hold her hand and she was scared. She said she was sorry." She looked at him. "She said it was Bert's fault. Do you think she was delirious?"

"Not really," he replied quietly.

"Why?"

"That can wait a bit." He grew somber. "You don't have any other family?"

She shook her head. She looked around. "But surely I can stay here by myself? I mean, I'm eighteen now…"

He frowned. "I thought you were seventeen."

She hesitated. Her eyes went to the calendar and she grimaced. "I just turned eighteen. Today is my birthday," she said. She hadn't even realized it, she'd been so busy. Tears ran down her cheeks. "What an awful one this is."

He caught her hand in his and held it tight. "No cousins?"

She shook her head. "I have nobody."

"Not quite true. You have me," he said firmly. "And Sara's on her way down here."

"Sara. Your sister?"

He nodded.

"She'll stay with me?" she asked.

He smiled. "Not exactly. "You'll stay with us, in my house. I won't risk your reputation by having you move in with just me."

"But…we're strangers," she pointed out.

"No, we're not," he said, and he smiled. "I told you about my stepfather. That's a memory I've never shared with anyone. And you won't mention it to Sara, right?"

"Of course not." She searched his black eyes. "Why would you do this for me?"

"Who else is there?" he asked.

She searched her mind for a logical answer and couldn't find one. She had nobody. Her best friend, Amy, had moved to New York City with her parents during the summer. They corresponded, and they were still friends, but Michelle didn't want to live in New York, even if

Amy's parents, with their five children, were to offer her a home.

"If you're thinking of the local orphanage," he said, tongue in cheek, "they draw the line at cow partisans."

She managed a laugh. "Oh. Okay."

"You can stay with us until you graduate and start college."

"I can't get in until fall semester, even if they accept me," she began.

"Where do you want to go?"

"Marist College in San Antonio. There's an excellent journalism program."

He pulled out his cell phone, punched a few buttons and made a phone call. Michelle listened with stark shock. He was nodding, laughing, talking. Then he thanked the man and hung up.

"You called the governor," she said, dumbfounded.

"Yes. We were in the same fraternity in college. He's on the board of trustees at Marist. You're officially accepted. They'll send a letter soon."

"But they don't have my grades...!"

"They will have, by the time you go. What's on the agenda for summer?" he continued.

"I... Well, I have a job. Minette Carson hired me for the rest of the school year, after school and on Saturdays. And I'm sure she'll let me work this summer, so I can save for college."

"You won't need to do that."

"What?"

He shrugged. "I drive a truck here because it helps me fit in. But I have an apartment in San Antonio with a garage. In the garage, there's a brand-new Jaguar XKE." He raised an eyebrow. "Does that give you a hint about my finances?"

She had no idea what an XKE was, but she knew what a Jaguar was. She'd priced them once, just for fun. If it was new…gosh, people could buy houses around here for less, she thought, but she didn't say it.

"But, I'm a stranger," she persisted.

"Not for long. I'm going to petition the court to become your temporary legal guardian. Sara will go with us to court. You can wear a dress and look helpless and tragic and in desperate need of assistance." He pursed his lips. "I know, it will be a stretch, but you can manage it."

She laughed helplessly.

"Then we'll get you through school."

"I'll find a way to pay you back," she promised.

He smiled. "No need for that. Just don't ever write about me," he added. It sounded facetious, but he didn't smile when he said it.

"I'd have to make up something in order to do that." She laughed.

She didn't know, and he didn't tell her, that there was more to his life than she'd seen, or would ever see. Sara knew, but he kept his private life exactly that—private.

Just for an instant, he worried about putting her in the line of fire. He had enemies. Dangerous enemies, who wouldn't hesitate to threaten anyone close to him. Of course, there was Sara, but she'd lived in Wyoming for the past few years, away from him, on a ranch they co-owned. Now he was putting her in jeopardy along with Michelle.

But what could he do? The child had nobody. Now that her idiot stepmother was dead, she was truly on her own. It was dangerous for a young woman to live alone, even in a small community. And there was Roberta's boyfriend, Bert.

Gabriel knew things about the man that he wasn't

eager to share with Michelle. The man was part of a criminal organization, and he knew Michelle's habits. He also had a yen for her, if what Michelle had blurted out to him once was true—and he had no indication that she would lie about it. He might decide to come and try his luck with her now that her stepmother was out of the picture. That couldn't be allowed.

He was surprised by his own affection for Michelle. It wasn't paternal. She was, of course, far too young for anything heavy, being eighteen to his twenty-four. She was a beauty, kind and generous and sweet. She was the sort of woman he usually ran from. No, strike that, she was no woman. She was still unfledged, a dove without flight feathers. He had to keep his interest hidden. At least, until she was grown up enough that it wouldn't hurt his conscience to pursue her. Afterward…well, who knew the future?

At the moment, however, his primary concern was to make sure she had whatever she needed to get through high school and, then, through college. Whatever it took.

Sara called him back. She wouldn't be able to get a flight to Texas for two days, which meant that Michelle would be on her own at night. Gabriel wasn't about to leave her, not with Bert Sims still out there. But he couldn't risk her reputation by having her stay alone with him.

"You don't want to be alone with me," Michelle guessed when he mentioned Sara's dilemma and frowned.

"It wouldn't look right," he said. "You have a spotless reputation here. I'm not going to be the first to put a blemish on it."

She smiled gently. "You're a very nice man."

He shrugged. "Character is important, regardless of the mess some people make of theirs in public and brag about it."

"My dad used to say that civilization rested on the bedrock of morality, and that when morality went, destruction followed," she recalled.

"A student of history," he said approvingly.

"Yes. He told me that first go the arts, then goes religion, then goes morality. After that, you count down the days until the society fails. Ancient Egypt. Rome. A hundred other governments, some more recently than others," she said.

"Who's right? I don't know. I like the middle of the road, myself. We should live the way that suits us and leave others to do the same."

She grinned. "I knew I liked you."

He chuckled. He finished his coffee. "We should stop discussing history and decide what to do with you tonight."

She stared at her own cooling coffee in the thick mug. "I could stay here by myself."

"Never," he said shortly. "Bert Sims might show up, looking for Roberta's leftovers, like Zack said."

She managed a smile. "Thanks. You could sleep in Roberta's room," she offered.

"Only if there's someone else in the house, too." He pursed his lips. "I have an idea." He pulled out his cell phone.

Carlie Blair walked in the door with her overnight bag and hugged Michelle close. "I'm so sorry," she said. "I know you and your stepmother didn't get along, but it's got to be a shock, to have it happen like that."

"It was." Michelle dashed away tears. "She apologized when she was dying. She said one other thing," she added, frowning, as she turned to Gabriel. "She said don't let Bert get away with it. You never told me what you thought that meant."

Gabriel's liquid black eyes narrowed. "Did she say anything else?"

She nodded slowly, recalling the odd statement. "She said he told her it wasn't pure and he lied. What in the world did that mean?"

Gabriel was solemn. "That white powder in the vial was cocaine," he explained. "Dealers usually cut it with something else, dilute it. But if it's pure and a user doesn't know, it can be lethal if they don't adjust the dose." He searched Michelle's eyes. "I'm betting that Bert gave her pure cocaine and she didn't know."

Carlie was surprised. "Your stepmother was using drugs?" she asked her friend.

"That's what they think," Michelle replied. She turned back to Gabriel. "Did he know it was pure? Was he trying to kill her?"

"That's something Zack will have to find out."

"I thought he cared about her. In his way," she faltered.

"He might have, even if it was only because she was a customer."

Michelle bit her lower lip. "That would explain why she was so desperate for money. I did wonder, you know, because she didn't buy new clothes or expensive cosmetics or things like she used to when Daddy was alive." She frowned. "She never bought anything, but she never had any money and she was always desperate for more. Like when she tried to sell my father's stamp collection."

"It's a very expensive habit," Gabriel said quietly.

"But…Bert might have meant to kill her…?"

"It's possible. Maybe she made threats, maybe she tried to quit or argued over the price. But, whether he meant to kill her or not, he's going to find himself in a lot of hot water pretty soon."

"Why?" Michelle asked curiously

He grimaced. "I'm sorry. That's all I can say. This is more complicated than it seems."

She sighed. "Okay. I won't pry. Keep your secrets." She managed a smile. "But don't you forget that I'm a reporter in training," she added. "One day, I'll have learned how to find out anything I want to know." She grinned.

"Now you're scaring me," he teased.

"Good."

He just shook his head. "I have to go back to my place and get a razor. I'll be right back. Lock the door," he told Michelle, "and don't open it for anybody. If Bert Sims shows up, you call me at once. Got that?"

"Got it," she said.

"Okay."

He left. Carlie got up from the sofa, where she'd been perched on the arm, and hugged Michelle. "I know this is hard for you. I'm so sorry."

"Me, too." Michelle gave way to tears. "Thanks for coming over. I hope I'm not putting you in any danger."

"Not me," Carlie said. "And neither of us is going to be in danger with that tall, dark, handsome man around. He is so good-looking, isn't he?" she added with a theatrical sigh.

Michelle dried her tears. "He really is. My guardian angel."

"Some angel."

She tried to think of something that might restore a little normalcy into her routine. Roberta was lying heavily on her mind. "I have to do dishes. Want to dry?"

"You bet!"

Chapter Five

Carlie and Michelle shared the double bed in Michelle's room, while Gabriel slept in Roberta's room. Michelle had insisted on changing the bed linen first. She put Roberta's clothes in the washing machine, the ones that had been scattered all over the room. When she'd washed them, she planned to donate them to charity. Michelle couldn't have worn them even if she'd liked Roberta's flamboyant style, which she didn't.

The next morning, Gabriel went to the local funeral home and made the arrangements for Roberta. She had an older sister in Virginia. The funeral home contacted her, but the woman wanted nothing to do with any arrangements. She and Roberta had never gotten along, and she couldn't care less, she said, whether they cremated her or buried her or what. Gabriel arranged for her to be cremated, and Reverend Blair offered a plot in the cemetery of his church for her to be interred. There would be

no funeral service, just a graveside one. Michelle thought
they owed her that much, at least.

Reverend Blair had invited Michelle to come and stay
at his house with Carlie, but Michelle wanted familiar
things around her. She also wanted Gabriel, on whom
she had come to rely heavily. But she couldn't stay with
Gabriel alone. It would not look right in the tiny community of Comanche Wells, where time hadn't moved
into the twenty-first century yet.

"Sara will be here tomorrow," Gabriel told the girls as
they sat down to supper, which Michelle and Carlie had
prepared together. He smiled as he savored hash browns
with onions, perfectly cooked, alongside a tender cut of
beef and a salad. "You two can cook," he said with ad-
miration. "Hash browns are hard to cook properly. These
are wonderful."

"Thanks," they said in unison, and laughed.

"She did the hash browns," Carlie remarked, grinning
at Michelle. "I never could get the hang of them. Mine
just fall apart and get soggy."

"My mother used to make them," Michelle said with
a sad smile. "She was a wonderful cook. I do my best,
but I'm not in her league."

"Where do your parents live, Gabriel?" Carlie asked
innocently.

Gabriel's expression went hard.

"I made a cherry pie for dessert," Michelle said,
quickly and neatly deflecting Carlie's question. "And
we have vanilla ice cream to go on it."

Carlie flushed, realizing belatedly that she'd made a
slight faux pas with her query. "Michelle makes the best
cherry pie around," she said with enthusiasm.

Gabriel took a breath. "Don't look so guilty," he told

Carlie, and smiled at her. "I'm touchy about my past, that's all. It was a perfectly normal question."

"I'm sorry, just the same," Carlie told him. "I get nervous around people and I babble." She flushed again. "I don't...mix well."

Gabriel laughed softly. "Neither do I," he confessed.

Michelle raised her hand. "That makes three of us," she remarked.

"I feel better," Carlie said. "Thanks," she added, intent on her food. "I have a knack for putting my foot into my mouth."

"Who doesn't?" Gabriel mused.

"I myself never put my foot into my mouth," Michelle said, affecting a haughty air. "I have never made a single statement that offended, irritated, shocked or bothered a single person."

The other two occupants of the table looked at her with pursed lips.

"Being perfect," she added with a twinkle in her eyes, "I am unable to understand how anyone could make such a mistake."

Carlie picked up her glass of milk. "One more word..." she threatened.

Michelle grinned at her. "Okay. Just so you remember that I don't make mistakes."

Carlie rolled her eyes.

It was chilly outside. Michelle sat on the porch steps, looking up at the stars. They were so bright, so perfectly clear in cold weather. She knew it had something to do with the atmosphere, but it was rather magical. There was a dim comet barely visible in the sky. Michelle had looked at it through a pair of binoculars her father had given her. It had been winter, and most hadn't been visible to the naked eye.

The door opened and closed behind her. "School is going to be difficult on Monday," she said. "I dread it. Everyone will know...you sure you don't mind giving me rides home after work?" she added.

"That depends on where you want to go," came a deep, amused masculine voice from behind her.

She turned quickly, shocked. "Sorry," she stammered. "I thought you were Carlie."

"She found a game show she can't live without. She's sorry." He chuckled.

"Do you like game shows?" she wondered.

He shrugged. He came and sat down beside her on the step. He was wearing a thick black leather jacket with exquisite beadwork. She'd been fascinated with it when he retrieved it from his truck earlier.

"That's so beautiful," she remarked, lightly touching the colorful trim above the long fringes with her fingertips. "I've never seen anything like it."

"Souvenir from Canada," he said. "I've had it for a long time."

"The beadwork is gorgeous."

"A Blackfoot woman made it for me," he said.

"Oh." She didn't want to pursue that. The woman he mentioned might have been a lover. She didn't want to think of Gabriel with a woman. It was intensely disturbing.

"My cousin," he said, without looking down at her. "She's sixty."

"Oh." She sounded embarrassed now.

He glanced at her with hidden amusement. She was so young. He could almost see the thoughts in her mind.

"You need somebody young to cut your teeth on, kid. They'd break on my thick hide."

She flushed and started to jump up, but he caught her hand in his big, warm one, and pulled her gently back down.

"Don't run," he said softly. "No problem was ever solved by retreat. I'm just telling you how it is. I'm not involved with anyone. I haven't been for years. You're a bud, just opening on a rosebush, testing the air and the sunlight. I like my roses in full bloom."

"Oh."

He sighed. His fingers locked into hers. "These one syllable answers are disturbing," he mused.

She swallowed. The touch of his big, warm hand was causing some odd sensations in her young body. "I see."

"Two syllables. Better." He drew in a long breath. "Until you graduate, we're going to be living in close proximity, even with Sara in the house. I'll be away some of the time. My job takes me all over the world. But there are going to have to be some strict ground rules when I'm home."

"Okay," she faltered. "What?"

"No pajamas or nightgowns when you walk around the house. You put them on when you go to bed, in your room. No staying up late alone. Stuff like that."

She blinked. "I feel like Mata Hari."

"You feel like a spy? An old one, at that." He chuckled.

"A femme fatale, then," she amended. "Gosh, I don't even own pajamas or a gown..."

"You don't wear clothes in bed?" He sounded shocked.

"Oh, get real," she muttered, glad he couldn't see her face. "I wear sweats."

"To bed?" he exclaimed.

"They're comfortable," she said. "Nobody who wanted

a good night's sleep ever wore a long gown, they just twist you up and constrict you. And pajamas usually have lace or thick embroidery. It's irritating to my skin."

"Sweats." Of all the things he'd pictured his young companion in at night, that was the last thing.

She looked down at his big hand in the light from the living room. It burned out onto the porch like yellow sun in the darkness, making shadows of the chairs behind them on the dusty boards of the porch. He had good hands, big and strong-looking, with square nails that were immaculate. "I guess the women you know like frilly stuff."

They did, but he wasn't walking into that land mine. He turned her hand in his. "Do you date?"

Her heart jumped. "Not since the almost-broken-nose thing."

He laughed softly. "Sorry. I forgot about that."

"There aren't a lot of eligible boys in my school who live in the dark ages like I do," she explained. "At least two of the ones who go to my church are wild as bucks and go to strip parties with drugs." She grimaced. "I don't fit in. Anywhere. My parents raised me with certain expectations of what life was all about." She turned to look at him. "Is it wrong, to have a belief system? Is it wrong to think morality is worth something?"

"Those are questions you should be asking Carlie's dad," he pointed out.

"Do you believe in...in a higher power?"

His fingers contracted around hers. "I used to."

"But not anymore?"

His drawn breath was audible. "I don't know what I believe anymore, *ma belle*," he said softly. "I live in a world you wouldn't understand, I go to places where you couldn't survive."

"What kind of work do you do?" she asked.

He laughed without humor. "That's a discussion we may have in a few years."

"Oh, I see." She nodded. "You're a cannibal."

He stilled. "I'm…a what?"

"Your work embarrasses you," she continued, unabashed, "which means you don't work in a bank or drive trucks. If I had a job that embarrassed me, it would be involved with cannibalism."

He burst out laughing. "Pest," he muttered.

She grinned.

His big thumb rubbed her soft fingers. "I haven't laughed so much in years, as I do with you."

She chuckled. "I might go on the stage. If I can make a hardcase like you laugh, I should be able to do it for a living."

"And here I thought you wanted to be a reporter."

"I do," she said. She smiled. "More than anything. I can't believe I'm actually going to work for a newspaper starting Monday," she said. "Minette is getting me my own cell phone and she's going to teach me to use a camera…it's like a dream come true. I only asked her for a reference for college. And she offered me a job." She shook her head. "It's like a dream."

"I gather you'll be riding with Carlie."

"Yes. I'm going to help with gas."

He was silent for a minute. "You keep your eyes open on the road, when you're coming home from work."

"I always do. But why?"

"I don't trust Roberta's boyfriend. He's dangerous. Even Carlie is in jeopardy because of what happened to her father, so you both have to be careful."

"I don't understand why someone would want to harm

a minister," she said, shaking her head. "It makes no sense."

He turned his head toward her. "Michelle, most ministers started out as something else."

"Something else?"

"Yes. In other words, Reverend Blair wasn't always a reverend."

She hesitated, listening to make sure Carlie wasn't at the door. "What did he do before?" she asked.

"Sorry. That's a confidence. I never share them."

She curled her hand around his. "That's reassuring. If I ever tell you something dreadful in secret, you won't go blabbing it to everyone you know."

He laughed. "That's a given." His hand contracted. "The reverse is also applicable," he added quietly. "If you overhear anything while you're under my roof, it's privileged information. Not that you'll hear much that you can understand."

"You mean, like when you were talking to Sara in French," she began.

"Something like that." His eyes narrowed. "Did you understand what I said?"

"I can say, where's the library and my brother has a brown suit," she mused. "Actually, I don't have a brother, but that was in the first-year French book. And it's about the scope of my understanding. I love languages, but I have to study very hard to learn anything."

He relaxed a little. He'd said some things about Michelle's recent problems to Sara that he didn't want her to know. Not yet, anyway. It would sound as if he were gossiping about her to his sister.

"The graveside service is tomorrow," she said. "Will Sara be here in time, do you think?"

"She might. I'm having a car pick her up at the airport and drive her down here."

"A car?"

"A limo."

Her lips parted. "A limousine? Like those long, black cars you see politicians riding around in on television? I've only seen one maybe once or twice, on the highway when I was on the bus!"

He laughed softly at her excitement. "They also have sedans that you can hire to transport people," he told her. "I use them a lot when I travel."

He was talking about another world. In Michelle's world, most cars were old and had plenty of mechanical problems. She'd never even looked inside a limousine. She'd seen them on the highway in San Antonio. Her father told her that important businessmen and politicians and rich people and movie stars rode around in them. Not ordinary people. Of course, Gabriel wasn't ordinary. He'd said he owned a new Jaguar. Certainly he could afford to ride in a limousine.

"Do you think they'd let me look inside, when it brings her here?" she asked.

Gabriel was amused at her innocence. She knew nothing of the world at large. He couldn't remember being that young, or that naive about life. He hoped she wouldn't grow up too quickly. She made him feel more masculine, more capable, more intriguing than he really was. He liked her influence. She made him laugh. She made him want to be all the things she thought he was.

"Yes," he said after a minute. "Certainly you can look inside."

"Something to put in my diary," she mused.

"You keep a diary?" he asked, with some amusement.

"Oh, yes," she said. "I note all the cows I've seen abducted, and the strange little men who come out of the pasture at night…"

"Oh, cool it." He chuckled.

"Actually, it's things like how I did on tests, and memories I have of my father and mother," she confessed. "And how I feel about things. There's a lot about Roberta and Bert in there, and how disgusting I thought they were," she added.

"Well, Roberta's where she can't hurt you. And Bert is probably trying to find a way out of the country, if he's smart."

"What do you mean?" she asked.

He stood up and pulled her up beside him. "That's a conversation for another time. Let's go see if Carlie's game show is off."

"Don't you like game shows?" she wondered aloud.

"I like the History Channel, the Nature Channel, the Military Channel, and the Science Channel."

"No TV shows?"

"They're not TV shows. They're experiments in how to create attention deficit disorders in the entire population with endless commercials and ads that pop up right in the middle of programs. I only watch motion pictures or DVDs, unless I find something interesting enough to suffer through. I like programs on World War II history and science."

She pondered that. "I guess there's five minutes of program to fifteen minutes of commercials," she agreed.

"As long as people put up with it, that will continue, too." He chuckled. "I refuse to be part of the process."

"I like history, too," she began.

"There was this big war…" he began with an exaggerated expression.

She punched his arm affectionately. "No cherry pie and ice cream for you."

"I take it back."

She grinned up at him. "Okay. You can have pie and ice cream."

He smiled and opened the door for her.

She hesitated in the opening, just staring up at him, drinking in a face that was as handsome as any movie star's, at the physique that could have graced an athlete.

"Stop ogling me, if you please," he said with exaggerated patience. "You have to transfer that interest to someone less broken."

She made a face at him. "You're not broken," she pointed out. "Besides, there's nobody anywhere who could compare with you." She flushed at her own boldness. "Anyway, you're safe to cut my teeth on, and you know it." She grinned. "I'm off-limits, I am."

He laughed. "Off-limits, indeed, and don't you forget it."

"Spoilsport."

She went inside ahead of him. He felt as if he could fly. Dangerous, that. More dangerous, his reaction to her. She was years too young for anything more than banter. But, he reminded himself, the years would pass. If he lived long enough, after she graduated from college, who knew what might happen?

There was a grim memorial service at the Comanche Wells Cemetery. It was part of the land owned by the Methodist church where Reverend Blair was the minister. He stood over the small open grave, with an open Bible in his hands, reading the service for the dead. The urn containing Roberta's ashes was in the open grave,

waiting for the funeral home's maintenance man, standing nearby, to close after the ceremony.

Gabriel stood beside Michelle, close, but not touching. He was wearing a suit, some expensive thing that fit
him with delicious perfection. The navy darkness of the
suit against the spotless white shirt and blue patterned
tie only emphasized his good looks. His wavy black hair
was unruly in the stiff breeze. Michelle's own hair was
tormented into a bun because of the wind. But it blew
tendrils down into her eyes and mouth while she tried to
listen to the service, while she tried even harder to feel
something for the late Roberta.

It was sad that the woman's own sister didn't care
enough to even send a flower. Total strangers from Jacobs
County had sent sprays and wreathes and potted plants
to the funeral home that had arranged for the cremation.
The flowers were spread all around the grave. Some of
them would go to the local hospital and nursing home in
Jacobsville, others for the evening church service here.
A few of the potted plants would go home with Michelle.

She remembered her father, and how much he'd been
in love with Roberta at first. She remembered Roberta
in the days before Bert. More recently, she remembered
horrible arguments and being slapped and having Roberta
try to sell the very house under her feet. There had been
more bad times than good.

But now that part of her life was over. She had a future that contained Gabriel, and the beginning of a career as a journalist. It was something to look forward to,
something to balance her life against the recent death of
her father and Roberta's unexpected passing.

Sara's plane had been held up due to an electrical fault.
She'd phoned Gabriel just before he and Michelle went to
the funeral with Carlie, to apologize and give an updated

arrival time. Michelle looked forward to meeting her. From what Gabriel had said about his sister, she sounded like a very sweet and comfortable person.

Reverend Blair read the final verses, closed the Bible, bowed his head for prayer. A few minutes later, he paused to speak to Michelle, where she stood with Gabriel and Carlie, thanking the few local citizens who'd taken time to attend. There hadn't been time for the newspaper to print the obituary, so services had been announced on the local radio station. Everybody listened to it, for the obituaries and the country-western music. They also listened for the school closings when snow came. That didn't happen often, but Michelle loved the rare times when it did.

"I'm sorry for your loss," Reverend Blair said, holding Carlie's hand and smiling gently. "No matter how contrary some people are, we get used to having them in our lives."

"That's true," Michelle said gently. "And my father loved her," she added. "For a time, she made him happy." She grimaced. "I just don't understand how she changed so much, so quickly. Even when she drank too much..." she hesitated, looking around to make sure she wasn't overheard before she continued, "she was never really mean."

Gabriel and the minister exchanged enigmatic glances.

Michelle didn't notice. Her eyes were on the grave. "And she said not to let Bert get away with it," she added slowly.

"There are some things going on that you're better off not knowing about," Reverend Blair said softly. "You can safely assume that Bert will pay a price for what he did. If not in this life, then in the next."

"But what did he do?" Michelle persisted.

"Bad things." Reverend Blair smiled.

"My sister will be here in an hour," Gabriel said, reading the screen of his cell phone, with some difficulty because of the sun's glare. He grinned at the reverend. "You can have your daughter back tonight."

Reverend Blair grinned. "I must say, I miss the little touches. Like clean dishes and laundry getting done." He made a face. "She's made me lazy." He smiled with pure affection at his daughter, who grinned.

"I'll make you fresh rolls for supper," Carlie promised him.

"Oh, my, and I didn't get you anything," he quipped.

She hugged him. "You're just the best dad in the whole world."

"Pumpkin, I'm glad you think so." He let her go. "If you need anything, you let us know, all right?" he asked Michelle. "But you're in good hands." He smiled at Gabriel.

"She'll be safe, at least." Gabriel gave Reverend Blair a complicated look. "Make sure about those new locks, will you? I've gotten used to having you around."

The other man made a face. "Locks and bolts won't keep out the determined," he reminded him. "I put my trust in a higher power."

"So do I," Gabriel replied. "But I keep a Glock by the bed."

"Trust in Allah, but tie up your camel."

Everybody looked at Michelle, who blushed.

"Sorry," she said. "I was remembering something I read in a nonfiction book about the Middle East. It was written by a former member of the French Foreign Legion."

Now the stares were more complicated, from the two males at least.

"Well, they fascinate me," she confessed, flushing a

little. "I read true crime books and biographies of military men and anything I can find about the Special Air Services of Great Britain and the French Foreign Legion."

"My, my," Gabriel said. He chuckled with pure glee, a reaction that was lost on Michelle.

"I lead a sheltered life." Michelle glanced at the grave. The maintenance man, a little impatient, had started to fill the grave. "We should go."

"Yes, we should." Reverend Blair smiled. "Take care."

"Thanks. The service was very nice," Michelle said.

"I'm glad you thought so."

Gabriel took her arm and led her back to the car. He drove her home first, so that she could change back into more casual clothes and get her overnight bag. Then he drove her to his own house, where Sara was due to arrive any minute.

Michelle had this picture of Sara. That she'd be dark-haired and dark-eyed, with a big smile and a very tender nature. Remembering what Gabriel had told her in confidence, about the perils Sara had survived when they were in school, she imagined the other woman would be a little shy and withdrawn.

So it came as something of a shock when a tall, beautiful woman with long black hair and flashing black eyes stepped out of the back of the limousine and told the driver where he could go and how fast.

Chapter Six

"I am very sorry, lady," the driver, a tall lanky man, apologized. "I truly didn't see the truck coming..."

"You didn't look!" she flashed at him in a terse but sultry tone. "How dare you text on your cell phone while driving a customer!"

He was very flushed by now. "I won't do it again, I swear."

"You won't do it with me in the car, and I am reporting you to the company you work for," she concluded.

Gabriel stepped forward as the driver opened the trunk. He picked up the single suitcase that Sara had brought with her. Something in the way Gabriel looked at the man had him backing away.

"Very sorry, again," he said, flustered. "If you'd just sign the ticket, ma'am..."

He fetched a clipboard and handed it to her, eyeing Gabriel as if he expected him to leap on him any second.

Sara signed it. The man obviously knew better than to look for a tip. He nodded, turned, jumped into the car and left a trail of dust as he sped away.

"That could have gone better," Sara said with a grim smile. She hugged Gabriel. "So good to see you again."

"You, too," he replied. His face changed as he looked at the younger woman. He touched her hair. "You only grow more beautiful with age."

"You only think so because you're my brother." She laughed musically. She looked past him at Michelle, who stood silent and wary.

"And you must be Michelle." Sara went to her, smiled and hugged her warmly. "I have a nasty temper. The silly man almost killed us both, texting some woman."

"I'm so glad he didn't," Michelle said, hugging her back. "It's very kind of both of you to do this for me," she added. "I...really don't have anyplace to go. I mean, the Reverend Blair said I could stay with him and Carlie, but..."

"You certainly do have someplace to go," Gabriel said with a grin. "Sara needed the change of scenery. She was vegetating up in Wyoming."

Sara sighed. "In a sense, I suppose so, although I like it better there than in British Columbia. I left our fore-man in charge at the ranch in Catelow. That's in Wyo-ming," Sara told Michelle with a smile. "Anything that needs doing for the sale, I can do online." Her black eyes, so like Gabriel's, had a sad cast. "The change of scenery will do me good. I love to ride. Do you?" she asked the younger woman.

"I haven't been on a horse in years," Michelle con-fessed. "Mostly, horses try to scrape me off or dislodge me. I'm sort of afraid of them."

"My horses are very tame," Gabriel told her. "They'll love you."

"I hope you have coffee made," Sara sighed as they made their way into the sprawling house. "I'm so tired! Flying is not my favorite mode of travel."

"I've never even been on a plane," Michelle confessed.

Sara stopped and stared at her. "Never?"

"Never."

"She wanted to look inside the limo." Gabriel chuckled. "She's never seen one of those, either."

"I'm so sorry!" Sara exclaimed. "I made a fuss…"

"You should have made a fuss," Michelle replied. "There will be other times."

"I'll make sure of that." Sara smiled, and it was like the sun coming out.

School had been rough in the days after Roberta's death. People were kind, but there were so many questions about how she died. Gossip ran rampant. One of the girls she sat near in history class told her that Roberta's boyfriend was a notorious drug dealer. At least two boys in their school got their fixes from him.

Now the things Roberta had said started to make sense. And Michelle was learning even more about the networks and how they operated from Minette since she'd started working for the Jacobsville newspaper.

"It's a vile thing, drug dealing," Minette said harshly. "Kids overdose and die. The men supplying the drugs don't even care. They only care about the profit." She hesitated. "Well, maybe some of them have good intentions…"

"A drug dealer with good intentions?" Michelle laughed. "You have got to be kidding."

"Actually, I'm not. You've heard of the man they call El Jefe?"

"Who hasn't?" Michelle replied. "We heard that he helped save you and Sheriff Carson," she added.

"He's my father."

Michelle gaped at her. "He's...?"

"My father," Minette repeated. "I didn't know who my real father was until very recently. My life was in danger, even more than Hayes's was when he was shot, because my father was in a turf war with a rival who was the most evil man I ever knew."

"Your life is like a soap opera," Michelle ventured.

Minette laughed. "Well, yes, it is."

"I wish mine was more exciting. In a good way," she clarified. She drew in a long breath. "Okay, what about this camera?" she asked. It had more dials and settings than a spaceship.

"I know, it's a little intimidating. Let me show you how it works."

She did. It took a little time, and when they finished, a phone call was waiting for Minette. She motioned to Michelle. "I have a new reporter. I'm going to let her take this down, if you don't mind. Her name is Michelle.... That's right. It's a deal. Thanks!" She put her hand over the receiver so that the caller wouldn't hear. "This is Ben Simpson. He's our Jacobs County representative in District 3 for the Texas Soil and Water Conservation Board. He wants us to do a story on a local rancher who won Rancher of the Year for the Jacobs County Soil and Water Conservation District for his implementation of natural grasses and ponds. The award was made just before Christmas, but the rancher has been out of the country until now. I'm going to let you take down the details, and then I'll send you out to his ranch to take a photo of him with the natural grasses in the background. Are you up to it?" she teased.

Michelle was almost shaking, but she bit her lip and nodded. "Yes, ma'am," she said.

Minette grinned. "Go for it!"

Michelle was used to taking copious notes in school. She did well in her schoolwork because she was thorough. She took down the story, pausing to clarify the spelling of names, and when she was through she had two sheets of notes and she'd arranged a day and time to go out to photograph the rancher.

She hung up. Minette was still in the doorway. "Did I do that okay?" she asked worriedly.

"You did fine. I was listening on the other phone. I took notes, too, just in case. You write the story and we'll compare your notes to mine."

"Thanks!" Michelle said fervently. "I was nervous."

"No need to be. You'll do fine." She indicated the computer at the desk. "Get busy." She smiled. "I like the way you are with people, even on the phone. You have an engaging voice. It will serve you well in this business."

"That's nice of you to say," Michelle said.

"Write the story. Remember, short, concise sentences, nothing flowery or overblown. I'll be out front if you need me."

She started to thank Minette again, but it was going to get tedious if she kept it up, so she just nodded and smiled.

When she turned in the story, she stood gritting her teeth while Minette read it and compared it with her own notes.

"You really are a natural," she told the younger woman. "I couldn't have done better myself. Nice work."

"Thank you!"

"Now go home," she said. "It's five, and Carlie will be peeling rubber any minute to get home."

Michelle laughed. "I think she may. I'll see you tomorrow, then. Do I go out to photograph the man tomorrow, too?"

"Yes."

Michelle bit her lip. "But I don't have a license or own a car…there's only Roberta's and she didn't leave it to me. I don't think she even had a will…and I can't ask Carlie to take off from work…." The protests came in small bursts.

"I'll drive you out there," Minette said softly. "We might drop by some of the state and federal offices and I'll introduce you to my sources."

"That sounds very exciting! Thanks!" She sounded relieved, and she was.

"One more thing," Minette said.

"Yes?"

"I'm printing the conservation story under your own byline."

Michelle caught her breath. "My first one. That's so kind of you."

"You'll have others. This is just the first." She grinned. "Have a good night."

"I will. Sara's making homemade lasagna. It's my favorite."

"Sara?"

"Gabriel's sister. She's so beautiful." Michelle shook her head. "The two of them have been lifesavers for me. I didn't want to have to pick up and move somewhere else. I couldn't have stayed here to finish school without them."

"Not quite true," Minette replied. "You could have

come to us. Even Cash Grier mentioned that they could make room for you, if you needed a place to stay."

"So many," Michelle said, shaking her head. "They hardly know me."

"They know you better than you think," was the reply. "In small communities like ours, there are no secrets. Your good deeds are noted by many."

"I guess I lived in the city for too long. Daddy had patients but no real friends, especially after Roberta came into our lives. It was just the three of us." She smiled. "I love living here."

"So do I, and I've been here all my life." She cocked her head. "Gabriel seems an odd choice to be your guardian. He isn't what you think of as a family man."

"He's not what he seems," Michelle replied. "He was kind to me when I needed it most." She made a face. "I was sitting in the middle of the road hoping to get hit by a car. It was the worst day of my life. He took me home with him and talked to me. He made everything better. When Roberta…died…he was there to comfort me. I owe him a lot. He even got Sara down here to live with him so that he could be my legal guardian with no raised eyebrows around us."

Minette simply said, "I see." What she did see, she wasn't going to share. Apparently Gabriel had a little more than normal interest in this young woman, but he wasn't going to risk her reputation. It was going to be all by the book. Minette wondered what he had in mind for Michelle when she was a few years older. And she also wondered if Michelle had any idea who Gabriel really was, and how he earned his living. That was a secret she wasn't going to share, either. Not now.

"Well, I'll see you tomorrow, then," Michelle added.

"Tomorrow."

* * *

Carlie was waiting for her at the front door the next morning, which was Friday. She looked out of breath.

"Is something wrong?" Michelle asked.

"No. Of course not. Let's go."

Carlie checked all around the truck and even looked under it before she got behind the wheel and started it.

"Okay, now, what's going on?" Michelle asked.

"Daddy got a phone call earlier," Carlie said, looking both ways before she pulled carefully out of the driveway.

"What sort of call?"

"From some man who said Daddy might think he was out of the woods, but somebody else was coming to pay him a visit, and he'll never see it coming." She swallowed. "Daddy told me to check my truck out before I drove it. I forgot, so I looked underneath just in case." She shook her head. "It's like a nightmare," she groaned. "I have no idea in this world why anyone would want to harm a minister."

"It's like our police chief said," Michelle replied quietly. "There are madmen in the world. I guess you can't ever understand what motivates them to do the things they do."

"I wish things were normal again," Carlie said in a sad tone. "I hate having to look over my shoulder when I drive and look for bombs under my car." She glanced at Michelle. "I swear, I feel like I'm living in a combat zone."

"I know the feeling, although I've never been in any real danger. Not like you." She smiled. "Don't you worry. I'll help you keep a lookout."

"Thanks." She smiled. "It's nice, having someone to ride with me. These back roads get very lonely."

"They do, indeed." Michelle sighed as she looked out

over the barren flat landscape toward the horizon as the
car sped along. "I just wrote my first story for the newspaper," she said with a smile. "And Minette is taking me
out to introduce me to people who work for the state and
federal government. It's the most exciting thing that's
ever happened to me," she added, her eyes starry with
pleasure. "I get my own byline." She shook her head. "It
really is true…"

"What's true?" Carlie asked.

"My dad said that after every bad experience, something wonderful happens to you. It's like you pay a price
for great happiness."

"I see what you mean." She paused. "I really do."

Minette drove Michelle out to the Patterson ranch, to
take photographs for her story and to see the rancher's
award for conservation management. She also wanted
a look at his prize Santa Gertrudis bull. The bull had
been featured in a cattle magazine because he was considered one of the finest of his breed, a stud bull whose
origins, like all Santa Gertrudis, was the famous King
Ranch in Texas. It was a breed native to Texas that had
resulted from breeding Shorthorn and Hereford cattle
with Brahman cattle. The resulting breed was named for
the Spanish land grant where Richard King founded the
cattle empire in the nineteenth century: Santa Gertrudis.

Wofford Patterson was tall, intimidating. He had jet-
black hair, thick and straight, and an olive complexion.
His eyes, surprisingly, were such a pale blue that they
seemed to glitter like Arctic ice. He had big hands and
big feet and his face looked as if it had been carved from
solid stone. It was angular. Handsome, in its way, but not
conventionally handsome.

There were scars on his hands. Michelle stared at them

as she shook his hand, and flushed when she saw his keen, intelligent eyes noting the scrutiny.

"Sorry," she said, although she hadn't voiced her curiosity.

"I did a stint with the FBI's Hostage Rescue Team," he explained, showing her the palms of both big hands. "Souvenirs from many rappels down a long rope from a hovering chopper," he added with a faint smile. "Even gloves don't always work."

Her lips fell open. This was not what she'd expected when Minette said they'd take pictures of a rancher. This man wasn't what he appeared to be.

"No need to look threatened," he told her, and his pale eyes twinkled as he shoved his hands into the pockets of his jeans. "I don't have arrest powers anymore." He scowled. "Have you done something illegal? Is that why you look intimidated?"

"Oh, no, sir," she said quickly. "It's just that I was listening for the sound of helicopters." She smiled vacantly.

He burst out laughing. He glanced at Minette. "I believe you said she was a junior reporter? You didn't mention that she was nuts, did you?"

"I am not nuts, I have read of people who witnessed actual alien abductions of innocent cows," she told him solemnly. But her eyes were twinkling, like his.

"I haven't witnessed any," he replied, "but if I ever do, I'll phone you to come out and take pictures."

"Would you? How kind!" She glanced at Minette, who was grinning from ear to ear. "Now about that conservation award, Mr. Patterson…"

"Mr. Patterson was my father," he corrected. "And he was Mister Patterson, with a capital letter. He's gone now, God rest his soul. He was the only person alive I was really afraid of." He chuckled. "You can call me Wolf."

"Wolf?"

"Wofford...Wolf," he said. "They hung that nickname on me while I worked for the Bureau. I have something of a reputation for tracking."

"And a bit more," Minette interrupted, tongue in cheek.

"Yes, well, but we mustn't put her off, right?" he asked in return, and he grinned.

"Right."

"Come on and I'll show you Patterson's Lone Pine Red Diamond. He won a 'bull of the year' award for conformation, and I'm rolling in the green from stud fees. He has nicely marbled fat and large—" he cleared his throat "—assets."

Minette glanced at Michelle and shook her head when Wolf wasn't looking. Michelle interpreted that as an "I'll tell you later" look.

The bull had his own stall in the nicest barn Michelle had ever seen. "Wow," she commented as they walked down the bricked walkway between the neat wooden stalls. There was plenty of ventilation, but it was comfortably warm in here. A tack room in back provided any equipment or medicines that might be needed by the visiting veterinarian for the livestock in the barn.

There were two cows, hugely pregnant, in two of the stalls and a big rottweiler, black as coal, lying just in front of the tack room door. The animal raised his head at their approach.

"Down, Hellscream," he instructed. The dog lay back down, wagging its tail.

"Hellscream?" Michelle asked.

He grinned. "I don't have a social life. Too busy with the bloodstock here. So in my spare time, I play World of Warcraft. The leader of the Horde—the faction that fights the Alliance—is Garrosh Hellscream. I really don't like him much, so my character joined the rebellion to throw him out. Nevertheless, he is a fierce fighter. So is my girl, there," he indicated the rottweiler. "Hence, the name."

"Winnie Kilraven's husband is a gaming fanatic," Minette mused.

"Kilraven plays Alliance," Wolf said in a contemptuous tone. "A Paladin, no less." He pursed his lips. "I killed him in a battleground, doing player versus player. It was very satisfying." He grinned.

"I'd love to play, but my husband is addicted to the Western Channel on TV when he's not in his office being the sheriff," Minette sighed. "He and the kids watch cartoon movies together, too. I don't really mind. But gaming sounds like a lot of fun."

"Trust me, it is." Wolf stopped in front of a huge, sleek red-coated bull. "Isn't he a beaut?" he asked the women, and actually sighed. "I'd let him live in the house, but I fear the carpets would never recover."

The women looked at each other. Then he laughed at their expressions, and they relaxed.

"I read about a woman who kept a chicken inside once," Michelle said with a bland expression. "I think they had to replace all the carpets, even though she had a chicken diaper."

"I'd like to see a cow diaper that worked." Wolf chuckled.

"That's a product nobody is likely to make," Michelle said.

"Can we photograph you with the bull?" Michelle asked.

"Why not?"

He went into the stall with the bull and laid his long arm around his neck. "Smile, Red, you're going to be even more famous," he told the big animal, and smoothed his fur.

He and the bull turned toward the camera. Michelle took several shots, showing them to Minette as they went along.

"Nice," Minette said. She took the digital camera, pulled up the shots, and showed them to Wolf.

"They'll do fine," Wolf replied. "You might want to mention that the barn is as secure as the White House, and anyone who comes here with evil intent will end up in the backseat of a patrol car, handcuffed." He pursed his lips. "I still have my handcuffs, just in case."

"We'll mention that security is tight." Minette laughed.

"He really is a neat bull," Michelle added. "Thanks for letting us come out and letting us take pictures."

He shrugged broad shoulders. "No problem. I'm pretty much available until next week."

"What happens next week?" Michelle asked.

"A World Event on World of Warcraft," he mused. "The 'Love Is in the Air' celebration. It's a hoot."

"A world event?" Michelle asked, curious.

"We have them for every holiday. It's a chance for people to observe them in-game. This is the equivalent of Valentine's Day." He laughed. "There's this other player I pal around with. I'm pretty sure she's a girl. We do battlegrounds together. She gets hung on trees, gets lost, gets killed a lot. I enjoy playing with her."

"Why did you say that you think she's a girl?" Michelle asked.

"People aren't what they seem in video games," he replied. "A lot of the women are actually men. They think of it as playing with a doll, dressing her up and stuff."

"What about women, do they play men?" she persisted.

He laughed. "Probably. I've come across a few whose manners were a dead giveaway. Women are mostly nicer than some of the guys."

"What class is your Horde character?" Minette broke in.

"Oh, you know about classes, huh?"

"Just what I overheard when Kilraven was raving about them to my husband," she replied, chuckling.

"I play a Blood Elf death knight," he said. "Two-handed sword, bad attitude, practically invincible."

"What does the woman play?" Michelle asked, curious.

"A Blood Elf warlock. Warlocks cast spells. Deadliest class there is, besides mages," he replied. "She's really good. I've often wondered where she lives. Somewhere in Europe, I think, because she's on late at night, when most people in the States are asleep."

"Why are you on so late yourself?" Michelle asked.

He shrugged. "I have sleep issues." And for an instant, something in his expression made her think of wounded things looking for shelter. He searched her eyes. "You're staying with the Brandons, aren't you?"

"Well, yes," she said hesitantly.

He nodded. "Gabriel's a good fellow." His face tautened. "His sister, however, could drop houses on people."

She stared at him. "Excuse me?"

"I was backing out of a parking space at the county courthouse and she came flying around the corner and hit the back end of my truck." He was almost snarling. "Then she gets out, cussing a blue streak, and says it's my fault! She was the one speeding!"

Michelle almost bit her tongue off trying not to say what she was thinking.

"So your husband—" he nodded to Minette "—comes

down the courthouse steps and she's just charming to him, almost in tears over her poor car, that I hit!" He made a face. "I get hit with a citation for some goldarned thing, and my insurance company has to fix her car and my rates go up."

"Was that before or after you called her a broom-riding witch and indicated that she didn't come from Wyoming at all, but by way of Kansas…?"

"Sure, her and the flying monkeys," he muttered.

Michelle couldn't keep from laughing. "I'm sorry," she defended herself. "It was the flying monkey bit…" She burst out laughing again.

"Anyway, I politely asked her which way she was going and if she was coming back to town, so I could park my truck somewhere while she was on the road. Set her off again. Then she started cussing me in French. I guess she thought some dumb country hick like me wouldn't understand her."

"What did you do?" Michelle asked.

He shrugged. "Gave it back to her in fluent and formal French. That made her madder, so she switched to Farsi." He grinned. "I'm also fluent in that, and I know the slang. She called on the sheriff to arrest me for obscenity, but he said he didn't speak whatever language we were using so he couldn't arrest me." He smiled blithely. "I like your husband," he told Minette. "He was nice about it, but he sent her on her way. Her parting shot, also in Farsi, was that no woman in North America would be stupid enough to marry a man like me. She said she'd rather remain single forever than to even consider dating someone like me."

"What did you say to her then?" Michelle wanted to know.

"Oh, I thanked her."

"What?" Minette burst out.

He shrugged. "I said that burly masculine women didn't appeal to me whatsoever, and that I'd like a nice wife who could cook and have babies."

"And?" Minette persisted.

"And she said I wanted a malleable female I could chain to the bed." He shook his head.

"What did you say about that?"

"I said it would be too much trouble to get the stove in there."

Michelle almost doubled up laughing. She could picture Sara trying to tie this man up in knots and failing miserably. She wondered if she dared repeat the conversation when she got home.

Wolf anticipated her. He shook his finger at her. "No carrying tales, either," he instructed. "You don't arm the enemy."

"But she's nice," she protested.

"Nice. Sure she is. Does she keep her pointed hat in the closet or does she wear it around the house?" he asked pleasantly.

"She doesn't own a single one, honest."

"Make her mad," he invited. "Then stand back and watch the broom and the pointy hat suddenly appear."

"You'd like her if you got to know her," Michelle replied.

"No, thank you. No room in my life for a woman who shares her barn with flying monkeys."

Michelle and Minette laughed all the way back to the office.

"Oh, what Sara's missing," Minette said, wiping tears of mirth from her eyes. "He's one of a kind."

"He really is."

"I wish I could tell her what he said. I wouldn't dare. She's already scored a limousine driver. I expect she could strip the skin off Wofford Patterson at ten paces."

"A limousine?"

Michelle nodded. "The driver was texting someone at the wheel and almost wrecked the car. She reported him to the agency that sent him."

"Good for her," Minette said grimly. "There was a wreck a few months ago. A girl was texting a girlfriend and lost control of the car she was driving. She killed a ten-year-old boy and his grandmother who were walking on the side of the road."

"I remember that," Michelle said. "It was so tragic."

"It's still tragic. The girl is in jail, pending trial. It's going to be very hard on her parents, as well as those of the little boy."

"You have sympathy for the girl's parents?" Michelle ventured.

"When you work in this business for a while, you'll learn that there really are two sides to every story. Normal people can do something impulsive and wrong and end up serving a life term. Many people in jail are just like you and me," she continued. "Except they have less control of themselves. One story I covered, a young man had an argument with his friend while he was skinning a deer they'd just killed in the woods. Impulsively, he stabbed his friend with the knife. He cried at his trial. He didn't mean to do it. He had one second of insanity and it destroyed his life. But he was a good boy. Never hurt an animal, never skipped school, never did anything bad in his life. Then he killed his best friend on an impulse that he regretted immediately."

"I never thought of it like that," Michelle said, dazed.

"Convicted felons have families," she pointed out.

"Most of them are as normal as people can be. They go to church, give to charity, help their neighbors, raise good children. They have a child do something stupid and land in jail. They're not monsters. Although I must confess I've seen a few parents who should be sitting in jail." She shook her head. "People are fascinating to me, after all these years." She smiled. "You'll find that's true for you, as well."

Michelle leaned back. "Well, I've learned something. I've always been afraid of people in jail, especially when they work on the roadways picking up trash."

"They're just scared kids, mostly," Minette replied. "There are some bad ones. But you won't see them out on the highways. Only the trusted ones get to do that sort of work."

"The world is a strange place."

"It's stranger than you know." Minette chuckled. She pulled up in front of the newspaper office. "Now, let's get those photos uploaded and cropped and into the galleys."

"You bet, boss," Michelle said with a grin. "Thanks for the ride, too."

"You need to learn to drive," Minette said.

"For that, you need a car."

"Roberta had one. I'll talk to Blake Kemp. He's our district attorney, but he's also a practicing attorney. We'll get him going on probate for you."

"Thanks."

"Meanwhile, ask Gabriel about teaching you. He's very experienced with cars."

"Okay," she replied. "I'll ask him." It didn't occur to her to wonder how Minette knew he was experienced with cars.

Chapter Seven

"No, no, no!" Gabriel said through gritted teeth. "Michelle, if you want to look at the landscape, for God's sake, stop and get out of the car first!"

She bit her lower lip. "Sorry. I wasn't paying attention."

The truck, his truck, was an inch away from going into a deep ditch.

"Put it in Reverse, and back up slowly," he instructed, forcing his voice to seem calm.

"Okay." She did as instructed, then put it in gear, and went forward very slowly. "How's this?"

"Better," he said. He drew in a breath. "I don't understand why your father never taught you."

Mention of her father made her sad. "He was too busy at first and then too sick," she said, her voice strained. "I wanted to learn, but I didn't pester him."

"I'm sorry," he said deeply. "I brought back sad memories for you."

She managed a faint smile. "It's still not that long since he, well, since he was gone," she replied. She couldn't bring herself to say "died." It was too harsh a word. She concentrated on the road. "This is a lot harder than it looks," she said. She glanced up in the rearview mirror. "Oh, darn."

He glanced behind them. A car was speeding toward them, coming up fast. The road was straight and clear, however. "Just drive," he told her. "He's got plenty of room to pass if he wants to."

"Okay."

The driver slowed down suddenly, pulled around them and gave her a sign that made her flush.

"And that was damned well uncalled for," Gabriel said shortly. He pulled out his cell phone, called the state highway police, gave them the license plate number and offered to press charges if they caught the man. "She's barely eighteen and trying to learn to drive," he told the officer he was speaking to. "The road was clear, he had room to pass. He was just being a jerk because she was female."

He listened, then chuckled. "I totally agree. Thanks."

He closed the cell phone. "They're going to look for him."

"I hope they explain manners to him. So many people seem to grow up without any these days," she sighed. She glanced at her companion. It had made him really angry, that other man's rudeness.

He caught her staring. "Watch the road."

"Sorry."

"What's wrong?"

"Nothing. I was just…well, it was nice of you, to care that someone insulted me."

"Nobody's picking on you while I'm around," he said with feeling.

She barely turned her head and met his searching black eyes. Her heart went wild. Her hands felt like ice on the wheel. She could barely get her breath.

"Stop that," he muttered, turning his head away. "You'll kill us both."

She cleared her throat. "Okay."

He drew in a breath. "You may be the death of me, anyway," he mused, giving her a covert glance. She was very pretty, with her blond hair long, around her shoulders, with that creamy complexion and those soft gray eyes. He didn't dare pay too much attention. But when she was fully grown, she was going to break hearts. His jaw tautened. He didn't like to think about that, for some reason.

"Now make a left turn onto the next road. Give the signal," he directed. "That's right. Look both ways. Good. Very good."

She grinned. "This is fun."

"No, fun is when you streak down the interstate at a hundred and twenty and nobody sees you. That's fun."

"You didn't!" she gasped.

He shrugged. "Jags like to run. They purr when you pile on the gas."

"They do not."

"You'll see." He smiled to himself. He already had plans for her graduation day. He and Sara had planned it very well. It was only a couple of months away. He glanced at his companion. She was going to be absolutely stunned when she knew what they had in mind.

* * *

The piece on Wofford Patterson ran with Michelle's byline, along with photos of his native grasses, his water conservation project and his huge bull. People she didn't even know at school stopped her in the hall to talk to her. And not only other students. Teachers paid her more attention, as well. She felt like a minor celebrity.

"I actually had someone to sit with at lunch," she told Sara, all enthusiasm, when she got home from school that day. "Mostly I'm always by myself. But one little article in the paper with my name and just look!"

Sara managed a smile. "It was well written. You did a good job. Considering the material you had to work with," she added with smoldering black eyes.

Then Michelle remembered. Wofford Patterson. Mortal enemy. Sara's nemesis.

"Sorry," she said, flushing.

"The man is a total lunatic," Sara muttered, slamming pans around as she looked for something to boil pasta in. Her beautiful complexion was flushed. "He backed into me and tried to blame me for it! Then he said I rode a broom and kept flying monkeys in the barn!"

Michelle almost bit through her lower lip. She couldn't laugh. She couldn't laugh...

Sara glanced at her, rolled her eyes, and dragged out a big pot. "You like him, I gather?"

"Well, he didn't accuse me of keeping flying monkeys," Michelle said reasonably. "He's very handsome, in a rough-cut sort of way, and he loves animals."

"Probably because he is one," Sara said under her breath.

"He has this huge rottweiler. You wouldn't believe what he calls her!"

"Have you seen my hammer?" Gabriel interrupted suddenly.

Both women turned.

"Don't you keep it in the toolbox?" Michelle asked.

"Yes. Where's my toolbox?" he amended.

The two women looked at each other blankly. Then Sara flushed.

"I, uh, had to find a pair of pliers to turn the water spigot on outside. Not my fault," she added. "You have big hands and when you turn the water off, I can't turn it back on. I took the whole toolbox with me so I'd have access to whatever I needed."

"No problem. But where is it?" Gabriel added.

"Um," Sara frowned. "I think I remember...just a sec." She headed out the back door.

"Don't, for God's sake, tell her the name of Patterson's dog!" Gabriel said in a rough whisper.

She stared at him. "Why?"

He gave her a speaking look. "Who do you think Patterson's unknown buddy in World of Warcraft is?" he asked patiently.

Her eyes widened with glee. "You mean, they're buddies online and they don't know it?"

"In a nutshell." He grinned. "Two lonely people who can't stand each other in person, and they're soul mates online. Let them keep their illusions, for the time being."

"Of course." She shook her head. "She'd like him if she got to know him."

"I know. But first impressions die hard."

Sara was back, carrying a beat-up brown toolbox. "Here." She set it down on the table. "Sorry," she added sheepishly.

"I don't mind if you borrow stuff. Just put it back, please." He chuckled.

reballs, colorful and rare. "I'll be in college.
eve it."

led. "You'll grow. College changes people. You
world in a different way when you've studied
like Western Civilization and math."

m not looking forward to the math," she sighed.
ple say college trig is a nightmare."

Only if you don't have a tutor."

"But I don't…"

He glanced down at her. "I made straight A's."

"Oh." She grinned. "Okay. Thanks in advance."

He stretched. "No problem. Maybe you'll do better at math than you do at driving."

She thumped his arm. "Stop that. I can drive."

"Sort of."

"It takes practice," she reminded him. "How can I practice if you're always too busy to ride in the truck with me?"

"You could ask Sara," he pointed out.

She glowered at him. "I did."

"And?"

"She's always got something ready to cook." She pursed her lips. "In fact, she has pots and pans lined up, ready, in case I look like I'm even planning to ask her to ride with me." Her eyes narrowed suspiciously. "I have reason to believe you've been filling her head with irrelevant facts about how many times I've run into ditches."

"Lies."

"It was only one ditch," she pointed out.

"That reminds me." He pulled out his cell phone and checked a text message. He nodded. "I have a professional driving instructor coming out to work with you, starting Saturday afternoon."

"Coward," she accused.

She shrugged. "Some
brained."

"Listen," he said,
body who speaks six lan
motely be called scatterbra
your mind all the time."

"What a nice way to put it. No
vorite brother!"

He gave Michelle a droll look.

"Well, if I had other brothers, you'd still
ite," Sara amended.

"Are we going to drive some more today?" M
asked him hopefully.

"Maybe tomorrow," he said after a minute. He forced
a smile. He left, quickly.

Michelle sighed. "I can't follow orders," she explained
while Sara put water on to boil and got out spaghetti.

"He's just impatient," Sara replied. "He always was,
even when we were kids." She shook her head. "Some
habits you never grow out of."

Michelle knew a lot about Sara, and her childhood.
But she was too kindhearted to mention any of what Gabriel had told her. She just smiled and asked what she
could do to help.

Graduation was only days away. So much had happened to Michelle that she could hardly believe how
quickly the time had gone by. Marist College had accepted her, just as Gabriel had told her. She was sched-
uled for orientation in August, and she'd already had a
conversation online with her faculty advisor.

"I'm so excited," she told Gabriel. They were sitting on
the front porch, watching a meteor shower. There were a

He grinned. "I don't teach."

"I thought you were doing very well, except for the nonstop cursing."

"I thought you were doing well, except for the nonstop near accidents."

She threw up her hands and sighed. "Okay. Just push me off onto some total stranger who'll have a heart attack if I miss a turn. His family will sue us and we'll end up walking everywhere…"

He held up a hand. "I won't change my mind. I can't teach you how to drive with any efficiency. These people have been doing it for a long time."

She gave in. "Okay. I'll give it a shot." She looked up at him. "You and Sara are coming to graduation, aren't you?"

He smiled down at her. "I wouldn't miss it for the whole world, *ma belle.*"

Her heart jumped up into her throat. She could walk on air, because Gabriel teased her in that deep, soft tone that he used only with her.

He touched her long hair gently. "You're almost grown. Just a few more years."

"I'm eighteen."

He let go of her hair. "I know." He turned away. She was eighteen years old. Years too young for what he was thinking of. He had to let her go, let her grow, let her mature. He couldn't hold her back out of selfishness. In a few years, when she was through college, when she had a good job, when she could stand alone—then, yes, perhaps. Perhaps.

"You're very introspective tonight," she remarked.

"Am I?" He chuckled. "I was thinking about cows."

"Cows?"

"It's a clear night. If a UFO were to abduct a cow, we would probably see it."

"How exciting! Let's go looking for them. I'll drive!"

"Not on your life, and don't you have homework? Finals are coming up, I believe?"

She made a face. "Yes, they are, and I can't afford to make a bad grade." She glanced at him. "Spoilsport."

He shrugged. "I want you to graduate."

She folded her hands on her jeans-clad thighs. "I've never told you how much I appreciate all you and Sara have done for me," she said quietly. "I owe you so much…"

"Stop that. We were happy to help."

It had just occurred to her that she was going away, very soon, to college. She was going to live in the dormitory there. She wouldn't live with Sara and Gabriel again. Her holidays would be spent with fellow students, if anyone even stayed on campus—didn't the campus close for holidays?

"I can see the wheels turning," he mused, glancing down at her. "You'll come to us for holidays and vacations," he said. "Sara and I will be here. At least until you're through college. Okay?"

"But Sara has a place in Wyoming—" she began.

"We have a place in Wyoming, and we have a competent manager in charge of it," he interrupted. "Besides, she likes it here in Texas."

"I did notice she was up very late last night on the computer," she said under her breath.

"New expansion on her game," he whispered. "She and her unknown pal are running battlegrounds together. She's very excited."

Michelle laughed softly. "We should probably tell her."

"No way. It's the first time I've seen her happy, really

happy, in many years," he said wistfully. "Dreams are precious. Let her keep them."

"I suppose it won't hurt," she replied. "But she's not getting a lot of sleep."

"She hasn't slept well in a long time, despite therapy and prescriptions. This gaming might actually solve a few problems for her."

"You think?"

"We can wait and see, at least." He glanced at his watch, the numbers glowing in the darkness. "I have some paperwork to get through. You coming in?"

"In just a minute. I do love meteor showers."

"So do I. If you like astronomy, we'll have to buy a telescope."

"Could we?" she asked enthusiastically.

"Of course. I'll see about it."

"I would love to look at Mars!"

"So would I."

"I would love to go there," she ventured.

He shrugged. "Not going to happen."

"It was worth a try."

He chuckled, ruffled her hair and went back inside.

Graduation day was going to be long and exciting. Michelle had gone to the rehearsal, which had to be held inside because it was pouring rain that day. She had hoped it wouldn't rain on graduation day.

Her gown and cap fit perfectly. She wasn't going to graduate with honors, but she was at least in the top 10 percent of her class. Her grades had earned her a small scholarship, which would pay for textbooks. She didn't want Gabriel and Sara to be out of pocket on her account, regardless of their financial worth.

Her gown was white. It made her look almost angelic,

with her long blond hair down to her waist, her peaches-and-cream complexion delicately colored, her gray eyes glittering with excitement.

She didn't see Gabriel and Sara in the audience, but that wasn't surprising. There was a huge crowd. They were able to graduate outside because the skies cleared up. They held the graduation ceremonies on the football field, with faculty and students and families gathered for the occasion.

Michelle accepted her diploma from the principal, grinned at some of her fellow students and walked off the platform. On the way down, she remembered what a terrifying future she was stepping into. For twelve years, she'd gone to school every day—well, thirteen years if you counted kindergarten. Now, she was free. But with freedom came responsibility. She had to support herself. She had to manage an apartment. She had to pay bills….

Maybe not the bills part, totally. She would have to force Gabriel and Sara to let her pay rent. That would help her pride. She'd go off to college, to strangers, to a dormitory that might actually be unisex. That was a scary thought.

She ran to Gabriel and Sara, to be hugged and congratulated.

"You are now a free woman." Sara chuckled. "Well, mostly. Except for your job, and college upcoming."

"If it's going to be a unisex dorm," Michelle began worriedly.

"It's not," Gabriel assured her. "Didn't you notice? It's a Protestant college. They even have a chaplain."

"Oh. Oh!" She burst out laughing, and flushed. "No, I didn't really notice, until I thought about having to share my floor with men who are total strangers."

"No way would that happen," Gabriel said solemnly,

and his dark eyes flashed. "I'd have you driven back and forth first."

"So would I," Sara agreed. "Or I'd move up to San Antonio, get an apartment and you could room with me."

Tears stung Michelle's cheeks. She was remembering how proud her father had been of her grades and her ambitions, how he'd looked forward to seeing her graduate. He should have been here.

"Now, now," Gabriel said gently, as if he could see the thoughts in her mind. He brushed the tears away and kissed her eyelids closed. "It's a happy occasion," he whispered.

She was tingling all over from the unexpectedly intimate contact. Her heart went wild. When he drew back, everything she felt and thought was right there, in her eyes. His own narrowed, and his tall, muscular body tensed.

Sara coughed. She coughed again, to make sure they heard her.

"Lunch," Gabriel said at once, snapping out of it. "We have reservations."

"At one of the finest restaurants in the country, and we still have to get to the airport."

"Restaurant? Airport?" Michelle was all at sea.

Gabriel grinned. "It's a surprise. Someone's motioning to you." He indicated a female student who was waving like crazy.

"It's Yvonne," Michelle told them. "I promised to have my picture taken with her and Gerrie. They were in my geography class. Be right back!"

They watched her go, her face alive with pleasure.

"Close call, masked man," Sara said under her breath.

He stuffed his hands into his slacks and his expression hardened.

"You have to be patient," Sara added gently, and touched his chest with a small hand. "Just for a little while."

"Just for years," he said curtly. "While she meets men and falls in love...."

"Fat chance."

He turned and looked down at her, his face guarded but full of hope.

"You know how she feels," Sara said softly. "That isn't going to change. But she has to have time to grow up, to see something of the world. The time will pass."

He grimaced and then drew in a breath. "Yes. I suppose so." He laughed hollowly. "Maybe in the meantime, I can work up to how I'm going to explain my line of work to her. Another hurdle."

"By that time, she'll be more likely to understand."

He nodded. "Yes."

She hugged him impulsively. "You're a great guy. She already knows it."

He hugged her back. "I'll be her best friend."

"You already are." She drew back, smiling. The smile faded and her eyes sparked with temper as she looked past him.

"My, my, did you lose your broom?" came a deep, drawling voice from behind Gabriel.

"The flying monkeys are using it right now," Sara snarled at the tall man. "Are you just graduating from high school, too?" she added. "And I didn't get you a present."

He shrugged. "My foreman's daughter graduated. I'm her godfather."

"So many responses come to mind. But choosing just one," she pondered for a minute. She pursed her full lips.

"Do you employ a full-time hit man, or do you have to manage with pickups?"

He raised his thick eyebrows. "Oh, full-time, definitely," he said easily, hands deep in his jean pockets. He cocked his head. "But he doesn't do women. Pity."

Sara was searching for a comeback when Michelle came running back.

"Oh, hi, Mr. Patterson!" she said with a grin. "How's that bull doing?"

"Eating all he can get and looking better by the day, Miss Godfrey," he replied, smiling. "That was a good piece you wrote on the ranch."

"Thanks. I had good material to work with."

Sara made a sound deep in her throat.

"What was that? Calling the flying monkeys in some strange guttural language?" Wolf asked Sara with wide, innocent eyes.

She burst out in Farsi, things that would have made Michelle blush if she understood them.

"Oh, my, what a thing to say to someone!" Wolf said with mock surprise. He looked around. "Where's a police officer when you need one?"

"By all means, find one who speaks Farsi," Sara said with a sarcastic smile.

"Farsi?" Jacobsville police chief Cash Grier strolled up with his wife, Tippy. "I speak Farsi."

"Great. Arrest her," Wolf said, pointing at Sara. "She just said terrible things about my mother. Not to mention several of my ancestors."

Cash glanced at Sara, who was glowering at Wolf, and totally unrepentant.

"He started it," Sara said angrily. "I do not ride a broom, and I have never seen a flying monkey!"

"I did, once," Cash said, nodding. "Of course, a man threw it at me…"

"Are you going to arrest her?" Wolf interrupted.

"You'd have to prove that she said it," Cash began.

"Gabriel heard her say it," Wolf persisted.

Cash looked at Gabriel. So did Sara and Michelle and Tippy.

"I'll burn the pasta for a week," Sara said under her breath.

Gabriel cleared his throat. "Gosh, I'm sorry," he said. "I wasn't paying attention. Would you like to say it again, and this time I'll listen?" he asked his sister.

"Collusion," Wolf muttered. He glowered at Sara. "I still have my handcuffs from my FBI days…"

"How very kinky," Sara said haughtily.

Cash turned away quickly. His shoulders were shaking.

Tippy hit him.

He composed himself and turned back. "I'm sorry, but I really can't be of any assistance in this particular matter. Congratulations, Michelle," he added.

"Thanks, Chief Grier," she replied.

"Why are you here?" Wolf asked the chief.

"One of my young brother-in-law's older gaming friends is graduating," he replied with a smile. "We came to watch him graduate." He shook his head. "He's awesome at the Halo series on Xbox 360."

"So am I," Wolf said with a grin. He glanced at Gabriel. "Do you play?"

Gabriel shook his head. "I don't really have time."

"It's fun. I like console games. But I also like…" Wolf began.

"The reservations!" Gabriel interrupted, checking his watch. "Sorry, but we've got a flight to catch. Graduation present," he added with a grin and a glance at Michelle. "See you all later."

"Sure," Wolf replied. He glanced at Sara and his eyes twinkled. "An airplane, huh? Having mechanical problems with the broom…?"

"We have to go, right now," Gabriel said, catching Sara before she could move toward Wolf.

He half dragged her away, to the amusement of the others.

"You should have let me hit him," Sara fumed as they sat comfortably in the business-class section of an aircraft bound for New Orleans. "Just one little slap…"

"In front of the police chief, who would have been obliged to arrest you," Gabriel pointed out. "Not a good thing on Michelle's graduation day."

"No." She smiled at Michelle, who looked as amused as Gabriel did. "Sorry. That man just rubs me the wrong way."

"It's okay," Michelle said. "I can't believe we're flying to New Orleans for lunch." She laughed, shaking her head. "I've never been on a plane before in my life. The takeoff was so cool!" she recalled, remembering the burst of speed, the clouds coming closer, the land falling away under the plane as she looked out the window. They'd given her the window seat, so that she had a better view.

"It was fun, seeing it through your eyes," Sara replied, smiling. "I tend to take it for granted. So does he." She indicated Gabriel, who laughed.

"I spend most of my life on airplanes, of one type or another," Gabriel confessed. "I must admit, my flights aren't usually this relaxed."

"You never did tell me what you do," Michelle said.

"I'm sort of a government contractor," he said easily.

"An advisor. I go lots of places in that capacity. I deal with foreign governments." He made it sound conventional. It really wasn't.

"Oh. Like businessmen do."

"Something like that," he lied. He smiled. "You have your first driving lesson tomorrow," he reminded her.

"Sure you wouldn't like to do it instead?" she asked. "I could try really hard to avoid ditches."

He shook his head. "You need somebody better qualified than I am."

"I hope he's got a good heart."

"I'm sure he'll be personable…"

"I hope he's in very good health," she amended.

Gabriel just chuckled.

They ate at a five-star restaurant downtown. The food was the most exquisite Michelle had ever tasted, with a Cajun spiced fare that teased the tongue, and desserts that almost made her cry they were so delicious.

"This is one of the best restaurants I've ever frequented," Gabriel said as they finished second cups of coffee. "I always stop by when I'm in the area." He looked around at the elegant decor. "They had some problems during Hurricane Katrina, but they've remodeled and regrouped. It's better than ever."

"It was delicious," Michelle said, smiling. "You guys are spoiling me rotten."

"We're enjoying it," Sara replied. "And there's an even bigger surprise waiting when we get home," she added.

"Another one? But this was the best present I've ever had! You didn't need to…"

"Oh, but we did," Gabriel replied. He leaned back in his chair, elegant in a navy blue jacket with a black turtleneck and dark slacks. Sara was wearing a simple black dress with pearls that made her look both expensive and beautiful. Michelle, in contrast, was wearing the only good dress she had, a simple sheath of off-white, with her mother's pearls. She felt dowdy compared to her companions, but they didn't even seem to notice that the dress was old. They made her feel beautiful.

"What is it?" Michelle asked suddenly.

She was met with bland smiles.

"Wait and see," Gabriel said with twinkling black eyes.

Chapter Eight

It was very late when they got back to the ranch. There, sitting in the driveway, was a beautiful little white car with a big red ribbon tied around it.

Michelle gaped at it. Her companions urged her closer.

She touched the trunk, where a sleek silver Jaguar emblem sat above the keyhole.

"It's a Jag," she stammered.

"It's not the most expensive one," Sara said quickly when Michelle gave them accusing glances. "In fact, it's a midrange automobile. But it's one of the safest cars on the road. Which is why we got it for you. Happy Graduation!"

She hugged Michelle.

"It's too much," Michelle stammered, touching the body with awe. She fought tears. "I never dreamed... Oh, it's so...beautiful!" She turned and threw herself into Sara's arms, hugging her close. "I'll take such good care of it! I'll polish it by the inch, with my own hands...!"

"Don't I get a hug, too? It was my idea," Gabriel said.

She laughed, turned and hugged him close. "Of course you do. Thank you! Gosh, I never dreamed you'd get me a car as a present!"

"You needed one," Gabriel said at the top of her head. "You have to be able to drive to work for Minette in the summer. And you'll need one to commute from college to home on weekends. If you want to come home that often," he added.

"Why would I want to stay in the city when I can come down here and ride horses?" she asked, smiling up at him. He was such a dish, she thought dreamily.

Gabriel looked back at her with dark, intent eyes. She was beautiful. Men would want her. Other men.

"Well, try it out," Sara said, interrupting tactfully. "I'll help you untie the ribbon."

"I'm never throwing the ribbon away!" Michelle laughed. "Oh. Wait!" She pulled out her cell phone and took a picture of the car in its bow.

"Stand beside it. We'll get one of you, too," Gabriel said, pulling out his own cell phone. He took several shots, smiling all the time. "Okay. Now get inside and try it out."

"Who's riding shotgun?" Michelle asked.

They looked worriedly at each other.

"It's too late to take it out of the driveway," Gabriel said finally. "Just start it up."

Michelle stood at the door. It wouldn't open.

"The key," Sara prompted Gabriel.

"The key. Duh." He chuckled. He dug it out of his pants pocket and handed it to Michelle. It was still warm from his body.

She looked at the fob in the light from the porch. "There's no key."

"You don't need one."

She unlocked the car and got inside. "There's no gear-shift!"

"See the start button?" Gabriel prompted. "Press it."

She did. Nothing happened.

"Hold down the brake with your foot and then press it," he added.

She did. The car roared to life. She caught her breath as the vents opened and the gearshift rose up out of the console. "Oh!" she exclaimed. She looked at the controls, at the instrument panel, at the leather seats. "Oh!" she said again.

Gabriel squatted by the door, on the driveway. "Its creator said something like, 'we will never come closer to building something that is alive.' Each Jaguar is unique. Each has its own little idiosyncrasies. I've been driving them for years, and I still learn new things about them. They purr when they're happy, they growl when they want the open road." He laughed self-consciously. "Well, you'll see."

She leaned over and brushed her soft mouth against his cheek, very shyly. "Thanks."

He chuckled and got to his feet. "You're welcome."

"Thanks, Sara," she called to the other woman.

"It was truly our pleasure." Sara yawned. "And now we really should get to bed, don't you think? Michelle has an early morning, and I'm quite tired." She hesitated. "Perhaps we should check to make sure the flying monkeys are locked up securely...?"

They both laughed.

The driving instructor's name was Mr. Moore. He had a small white round patch of hair at the base of his skull. Michelle wondered if his hair loss was from close calls by students.

He was very patient. She had a couple of near-misses, but was able to correct in time and avoid an accident. He told her that it was something that much practice would fix. She only needed to drive, and remember her lessons.

So she drove. But it was Sara, not Gabriel, who rode with her that summer. Gabriel had packed a bag, told the women goodbye, and rushed out without another word.

"Where is he going?" Michelle had asked Sara.

The other woman smiled gently. "We're not allowed to know. Some of what he does is classified. And you must never mention it to anyone. Okay?"

"Of course not," Michelle replied. She bit her lip. "What he does—it's just office stuff, right? I mean he advises. That's talking to people, instructing, right?"

Sara hesitated only a beat before she replied, "Of course."

Michelle put it out of her mind. Gabriel didn't phone home. He'd been gone several weeks. During that time, Michelle began to perfect her driving skills, with Sara's help. She got her driver's license, passing the test easily, and now she drove alternately to work with Carlie.

"This is just so great," Carlie enthused on the way to work. "They bought you a Jaguar! I can't believe it!" She sighed, smoothing her hand over the soft leather seat. "I wish somebody would buy me a Jaguar."

Michelle chuckled. "It was a shock to me, too, let me tell you. I tried to give it back, but they wouldn't hear of it. They said I needed something safe. Like a big Ford truck wouldn't be safe?" she mused.

"I'd love a big brand-new Ford truck," Carlie sighed. "One of those F-Series ones. Or a Dodge Ram. Or a Chevy Silverado. I've never met a truck I didn't love."

"I like cars better," Michelle said. "Just a personal

preference." She glanced at her friend. "I'm going to miss riding with you when I go to college."

"I'll miss you, too." Carlie glanced out the window. "Just having company keeps me from brooding."

"Carson is still giving you fits, I gather?" Michelle asked gently.

Carlie looked down at her hands. "I don't understand why he hates me so much," she said. "I haven't done anything to him. Well, except make a few sarcastic comments, but he starts it," she added with a scowl.

"Maybe he likes you," Michelle ventured. "And he doesn't want to."

"Oh, sure, that's the reason." She shook her head. "No. That isn't it. He'd throw me to the wolves without a second thought."

"He spends a lot of time in Cash Grier's office."

"They're working on something. I'm not allowed to know what, and the chief makes sure I can't overhear him when he talks on the phone." She frowned. "My father's in there a lot, too. I can't imagine why. Carson isn't the praying sort," she added coldly, alluding to her father's profession. He was, after all, a minister.

"I wouldn't think the chief is the praying sort, either," Michelle replied. "Maybe it's something to do about that man who attacked your father."

"I've wondered about that," her companion replied. "Dad won't tell me anything. He just clams up if I mention it."

"You could ask the chief."

Carlie burst out laughing. "You try it," she replied with a grin. "He changes the subject, picks up the phone, drags someone passing by into the office to chat—he's a master at evasion."

"You might try asking Carson," she added.

The smile faded. "Carson would walk all over me."

"You never know."

"I know, all right." Carlie flushed a little, and stared out the window again.

"Sorry," Michelle said gently. "You don't want to talk about him. I understand."

"It's okay." She turned her head. "Is Gabriel coming back soon?"

"We don't know. We don't even know where he is," Michelle said sadly. "Some foreign country, I gather, but he didn't say." She shook her head. "He's so mysterious."

"Most men are." Carlie laughed.

"At least what he does is just business stuff," came the reply. "So we don't have to worry about him so much."

"A blessing," Carlie agreed.

Michelle did a story about the local fire department and its new fire engine. She learned a lot from the fire chief about how fires were started and how they were fought. She put it all into a nice article, with photos of the firemen. Minette ran it on the front page.

"Favoritism," Cash Grier muttered when she stopped by to get Carlie for the drive home that Friday afternoon.

"Excuse me?" Michelle asked him.

"A story about the fire department, on the front page," he muttered. He glared at her. "You haven't even done one about us, and we just solved a major crime!"

"A major crime." Michelle hadn't heard of it.

"Yes. Someone captured old man Jones's chicken, put it in a doll dress, and tied it to his front porch." He grinned. "We captured the perp."

"And?" Michelle prompted. Carlie was listening, too.

"It was Ben Harris's granddaughter." He chuckled. "Her grandmother punished her for overfilling the bathtub by taking away her favorite dolly. So there was this nice red hen right next door. She took the chicken inside, dressed it up, and had fun playing with it while her grandparents were at the store. Then she realized how much more trouble she was going to be in when they noticed what the chicken did, since it wasn't wearing a diaper."

Both women were laughing.

"So she took the chicken back to Jones' house, but she was afraid it might run off, so she tied it to the porch rail." He shook his head. "The doll's clothes were a dead giveaway. She's just not cut out for a life of crime."

"What did Mr. Jones do?" Michelle asked.

"Oh, he took pictures," he replied. "Want one? They're pretty cool. I'm thinking of having one blown up for my office. To put on my solved-crime wall." He grinned.

They were laughing so hard, tears were rolling down their cheeks.

"And the little girl?" Michelle persisted.

"She's assigned to menial chores for the next few days. At least, until all the chicken poop has been cleaned off the floors and furniture. They did give her back the doll, however," he added, tongue in cheek. "To prevent any future lapses. Sad thing, though."

"What is?"

"The doll is naked. If she brings it out of the house, as much as I hate it, I'll have to cite it for indecent exposure…"

The laughter could be heard outside the door now. The tall man with jet-black hair hanging down to his waist wasn't laughing.

He stopped, staring at the chief and his audience.

"Something?" Cash asked, suddenly all business.

"Something." Carson's black eyes slid to Carlie's face and narrowed coldly. "If you can spare the time."

"Sure. Come on in."

"If you don't need me, I'll go home," Carlie said at once, flushed, as she avoided Carson's gaze.

"I don't need you." Carson said it with pure venom.

She lifted her chin pugnaciously. "Thank God," she said through her teeth.

He opened his mouth, but Cash intervened. "Go on home, Carlie," he said, as he grabbed Carson by the arm and steered him into the office.

"So that's Carson," Michelle said as she drove toward Carlie's house.

"That's Carson."

Michelle drew in a breath. "A thoroughly unpleasant person."

"You don't know the half of it."

"He really has it in for you."

Carlie nodded. "Told you so."

There really didn't seem to be anything else to say. Michelle gave her a sympathetic smile and kept her silence until they pulled up in front of the Victorian house she shared with her father.

"Thanks for the ride," Carlie said. "My turn to drive tomorrow."

"And my turn to buy gas." She chuckled.

"You don't hear me arguing, do you?" Carlie sighed, smiling. "Gas is outrageously high."

"So is most everything else. Have a good night. I'll see you tomorrow."

"Sure. Thanks again."

Michelle parked her car in front of the house, noted that she really needed to take it through the car wash, and started toward the front door. Sara's car was missing. She hadn't mentioned being away. Not a problem, however, since Michelle had a key.

She started to put it into the lock, just as it opened on its own. And there was Gabriel, tanned and handsome and smiling.

"Gabriel!" She threw herself into his arms, to be lifted, and hugged, and swung around once, twice, three times, in an embrace so hungry that she never wanted to be free again.

"When did you get home?" she asked at his ear.

"About ten minutes ago," he murmured into her neck. "You smell of roses."

"New perfume. Sara bought it for me." She drew back just enough to see his face, her arms still around his neck, his arms still holding her close. She searched his eyes at point-blank range and felt her heart go into overdrive. She could barely breathe. He felt like heaven in her arms. She looked at his mouth, chiseled, perfect, and wondered, wondered so hard, how it would feel if she moved just a little, if she touched her lips to it…

His hand caught in her long hair and pulled. "No," he said through his teeth.

She met his eyes. She saw there, or thought she saw, the same burning hunger that was beginning to tauten her young body, to kindle needs she'd never known she had.

Her lips parted on a shaky breath. She stared at him. He stared back. There seemed to be no sound in the world, nothing except the soft rasp of her breathing and the increasing heaviness of his own. Against her flattened breasts, she could feel the warm hardness of his chest, the thunder of his heartbeat.

One of his hands slid up and down her spine. His black eyes dropped to her mouth and lingered there until she almost felt the imprint of them, like a hard, rough kiss. Her nails bit into him where her hands clung.

She wanted him. He could feel it. She wanted his mouth, his hands, his body. Her breath was coming in tiny gasps. He could feel her heartbeat behind the soft, warm little breasts pressed so hard to his chest. Her mouth was parted, moist, inviting. He could grind his own down into it and make her moan, make her want him, make her open her arms to him on the long, soft sofa that was only a few steps away....

She was eighteen. She'd never lived. There hadn't been a serious romance in her young life. He could rob her of her innocence, make her a toy, leave her broken and hurting and old.

"No," he whispered. He forced himself to put her down. He held her arms, tightly, until he could force himself to let go and step back.

She was shaky. She felt his hunger. He wasn't impervious to her. But he was cautious. He didn't want to start anything. He was thinking about her age. She knew it.

"I won't...always be eighteen," she managed.

He nodded, very slowly. "One day," he promised. "Perhaps."

She brightened. It was like the sun coming out. "I'll read lots of books."

His eyebrows arched.

"You know. On how to do...stuff. And I'll buy a hope chest and fill it up with frothy little black things."

The eyebrows arched even more.

"Well, it's a hope chest. As in, I hope I'll need it one day when you think I'm old enough." She pursed her lips and her gray eyes twinkled. "I could fake my ID...."

"Give it up." He chuckled.

She shrugged. "I'll grow up as fast as I can," she promised. She glowered at him. "I won't like it if I hear about you having orgies with strange women."

"Most women are strange," he pointed out.

She hit his chest. "Not nice."

"How's the driving?" he asked, changing the subject.

"I haven't hit a tree, run off the road or approached a ditch since you left," she said smugly. "I haven't even dinged the paint."

"Good girl," he said, chuckling. "I'm proud of you. How's the job coming along?"

"It's great! I'm working on this huge story! It may have international implications!"

Odd, how worried he looked for a few seconds. "What story?"

"It involves a kidnapping," she continued.

He frowned.

"A chicken was involved," she added, and watched his face clear and become amused. "A little girl whose doll was taken away for punishment stole a chicken and dressed it in doll's clothes. I understand she'll be cleaning the house for days to come."

He laughed heartily. "The joys of small-town reporting," he mused.

"They never end. How was your trip?"

"Long," he said. "And I'm starving."

"Sara made a lovely casserole. I'll heat you up some."

He sat down at the kitchen table and watched her work. She made coffee and put a mug of it, black, at his place while she dealt with reheating the chicken casserole.

She warmed up a piece of French bread with butter to go with it. Then she sat down and watched him eat while she sipped her own coffee.

"It sure beats fried snake," he murmured.

She blinked. "What?"

"Well, we eat what we can find. Usually, it's a snake. Sometimes, if we're lucky, a big bird or some fish."

"In an office building?" she exclaimed.

He glanced at her with amusement. "It's not always in an office building. Sometimes we have to go out and look at…projects, wherever they might be. This time, it was in a jungle."

"Wow." She was worried now. "Poisonous snakes?"

"Mostly. It doesn't really affect the taste," he added.

"You could get bitten," she persisted.

"I've been bitten, half a dozen times," he replied easily. "We always carry antivenin with us."

"I thought you were someplace safe."

He studied her worried face and felt a twinge of guilt. "It was just this once," he lied, and he smiled. "What I do is rarely dangerous." Another lie. A bigger one. "Nothing to concern you. Honest."

She propped her face in her hands, her elbows on the table, and watched him finish his meal and his coffee.

"Stop that," he teased. "I can take care of myself. I've been doing it for twenty-odd years."

She grimaced. "Okay. Just checking."

"I promise not to get killed."

"If you do, I'm coming after you. Boy, will you be sorry, too."

He laughed. "I hear you."

"Want dessert? We have a cherry pie."

He shook his head. "Maybe later. Where's Sara?"

"I have no idea. She didn't even leave a note."

He pulled out his cell phone and pressed the speed dial. He got up and poured more coffee into his cup while he waited.

"Where are you?" he asked after a minute.

There was a reply. He glanced at Michelle, his lips pursed, his eyes twinkling. "Yes, she's right here."

Another silence. He sat back down. He was nodding.

"No, I think it's a very good idea. But you might have asked for my input first....No, I agree, you have exquisite taste....Yes, that's true, returns are possible. I won't tell her. How long?...Okay. See you then." He smiled. "Me, too. Thanks."

He hung up.

"Where is she?" she asked.

"On her way home. With a little surprise."

"Something for me?" she asked, and her face brightened.

"I'd say so."

"But you guys have already given me so much," she began, protesting.

"You can take that up with my sister," he pointed out. "Not that it will do you much good. She's very stubborn."

She laughed. "I noticed." She paused. "What is it?"

"You'll have to wait and see."

Sara pulled up into the driveway and got out of her car. She popped the truck and dragged out several big shopping bags. She handed some to Gabriel and one to Michelle. She was grinning from ear to ear.

"What in the world...?" Michelle exclaimed.

"Just a few little odds and ends that you're going to need to start college. Come on inside and I'll show you. Gabriel, get your nose out of that bag, it's private!"

He laughed and led the way into the house.

Michelle was speechless. Sara had exquisite taste in clothing, and it showed in the items she'd purchased for their houseguest. There was everything from jeans and sweats to dresses and handbags and underwear, gossamer gowns and an evening gown that brought tears to Michelle's eyes because it was the loveliest thing she'd ever seen.

"You like them?" Sara asked, a little worried.

"I've never had things like this," she stammered. "Daddy was so sick that he never thought of shopping with me. And when Roberta took me, it was just for bras and panties, never for nice clothes." She hugged Sara impulsively. "Thank you. Thank you so much!"

"You might try on that gown. I wasn't sure about the size, but we can exchange it if it doesn't fit. I'll go have coffee with Gabriel while you check the fit." She smiled, and left Michelle with the bags.

They were sipping coffee in the kitchen when Michelle came nervously to the doorway. She'd fixed her hair, put on shoes and she was wearing the long, creamy evening gown with its tight fit and cap sleeves, revealing soft cleavage. There was faint embroidery on the bodice and around the hem. The off-white brought out the highlights in Michelle's long, pale blond hair, and accentuated her peaches-and-cream complexion. In her softly powdered face, her gray eyes were exquisite.

Gabriel turned his head when he caught movement in his peripheral vision. He sat like a stone statue, just staring. Sara followed his gaze, and her face brightened.

"It's perfect!" she exclaimed, rising. "Michelle, it's absolutely perfect! Now you have something to wear to a really formal occasion."

"Thanks," she replied. "It's the most beautiful thing I've ever owned." She glanced at Gabriel, who hadn't spoken. His coffee cup was suspended in his hand in midair, as if he'd forgotten it. "Does it…look okay?" she asked him, wanting reassurance.

He forced his eyes away. "It looks fine." He put the mug down and got to his feet. "I need to check the livestock." He went out the back door without a glance behind him.

Michelle felt wobbly. She bit her lower lip. "He didn't like it," she said miserably.

Sara touched her cheek gently. "Men are strange. They react in odd ways. I'm sure he liked it, but he's not demonstrative." She smiled. "Okay?"

Michelle relaxed. "Okay."

Out in the barn, Gabriel was struggling to regain his composure. He'd never seen anything in his life more beautiful than Michelle in that dress. He'd had to force himself out the door before he reacted in a totally inappropriate way. He wanted to sweep her up in his arms and kiss her until her mouth went numb. Not a great idea.

He stood beside one of his horses, stroking its muzzle gently, while he came to grips with his hunger. It was years too soon. He would have to manage the long wait. Meanwhile, he worried about the other men, young men, who would see Michelle in that gown and want her, as he wanted her. But they would be her age, young and untried, without his jaded past. They would be like her, full of passion for life.

It wasn't fair of him to try to keep her. He must distance himself from her, give her the chance to grow away from him, to find someone more suitable. It was going to be hard, but he must manage it. She deserved the chance.

* * *

The next morning, he was gone when Michelle went into the kitchen to help Sara fix breakfast.

"His truck's gone," Michelle said, her spirits dropping hard.

"Yes. I spoke to him late last night," Sara replied, not looking at her. "He has a new job. He said he might be away for a few weeks." She glanced at the younger woman and managed a smile. "Don't worry about him. He can take care of himself."

"I'm sure he can. It's just…" She rested her hand on the counter. "I miss him, when he's away."

"I'm sure you do." She hesitated. "Michelle, you haven't started to live yet. There's a whole world out there that you haven't even seen."

Michelle turned, her eyes old and wise. "And you think I'll find some young man who'll sweep me off my feet and carry me off to a castle." She smiled. "There's only one man I'll ever want to do that, you know."

Sara grimaced. "There are so many things you don't know."

"They won't matter," Michelle replied very quietly. She searched Sara's eyes. "None of it will matter."

Sara couldn't think of the right words. So she just hugged Michelle instead.

Chapter Nine

Michelle was very nervous. It was the first day of the semester on campus, and even with a map, it was hard to find all her classes. Orientation had given the freshmen an overview of where everything was off the quad, but it was so confusing.

"Is Western Civilization in Sims Hall or Waverly Hall?" she muttered to herself, peering at the map.

"Waverly," came a pleasant male voice from just behind her. "Come on, I'll walk you over. I'm Randy. Randy Miles."

"Michelle Godfrey," she said, shaking his hand and smiling. "Thanks. Are you in my class?"

He shook his head. "I'm a junior."

"Should you be talking to me?" she teased. "After all, I'm pond scum."

He stopped and smiled. He had dark hair and pale

eyes. He was a little pudgy, but nice. "No. You're not pond scum. Trust me."

"Thanks."

"My pleasure. Are you from San Antonio?"

"My family is from Jacobsville, but I lived here with my parents while they were alive."

"Sorry."

"They were wonderful people. The memories get easier with time." She glanced around. "This is a huge campus."

"They keep adding to it," he said. "Sims Hall is brandnew. Waverly is old. My father had history with old Professor Barlane."

"Really?"

He nodded. "Just a word of warning, never be late for his class. You don't want to know why."

She grinned. "I'll remember."

On the way to Waverly Hall, Randy introduced Michelle to two of his friends, Alan Drew and Marjory Wills. Alan was distantly pleasant. Marjory was much more interested in talking to Randy than being introduced to this new student.

"You're going to be late for class, aren't you?" Alan asked Michelle, checking his watch. "I'll walk you the rest of the way."

"Nice to have met you," Randy said pleasantly. Marjory just nodded.

Michelle smiled and followed Alan to the towering building where her class was located.

"Thanks," she said.

He shrugged and smiled. "Those two." He rolled his eyes. "They're crazy about each other, but neither one will admit it. Don't let them intimidate you, especially Marjory. She has...issues."

"No problem. I guess I'll see you around."

"You will." He leaned forward, grinning. "I'm in the class you're going to right now. And we'd better hurry!"

They barely made it before the bell. The professor, Dr. Barlane, was old and cranky. He gave the class a dismissive look and began to lecture. Michelle was grateful that she'd learned how to take notes, because she had a feeling that this class was going to be one of the more demanding ones.

Beside her, Alan was scribbling on scraps of paper instead of a notebook, like Michelle. He wasn't bad-looking. He had dark hair and eyes and a nice smile, but in her heart, there was only Gabriel. She might like other men as friends, but there was never going to be one to compare with Gabriel.

After class, Alan left her with a smile and whistled as he continued on to his next class. Michelle looked at her schedule, puzzled out the direction to go and went along the walkway to the next building.

"Well, how was it?" Sara asked that night on the phone.

"Very nice," she replied. "I made a couple of friends."

"Male ones?" Sara teased.

"What was that?" Gabriel spoke up in the background.

"She made friends," Sara called to him. "Don't have a cow."

He made a sarcastic sound and was quiet.

"How do you like your roommate?" Sara continued.

Michelle glanced into the next room, where Darla was searching frantically for a blouse she'd unpacked and couldn't find, muttering and ruffling her red hair.

"She's just like me. Disorganized and flighty," Michelle said, a little loudly.

"I heard that!" Darla said over her shoulder.

"I know!" Michelle laughed. Darla shook her head, laughing, too.

"We're going to get along just fine," Michelle told Sara. "Neither of us has half a mind, and we're so disorganized that we're likely to be thrown out for creating a public eyesore."

"Not likely," Sara replied. "Well, I'm glad things are going well. If you need us, you know where we are, sweetie."

"I do. Thanks. Thanks for everything."

"Keep in touch. Good night."

"Good night."

"Your family?" Darla asked, poking her head into the room.

Michelle hesitated, but only for a second. She smiled. "Yes. My family."

Michelle adjusted to college quite easily. She made some friends, mostly distant ones, and one good one—her roommate, Darla. She and Darla were both religious, so they didn't go to boozy parties or date promiscuous boys. That meant they spent a lot of time watching rented movies and eating popcorn in their own dorm room.

One thing Sara had said was absolutely true; college changed her. She learned things that questioned her own view of the world and things about other cultures. She saw the rise and fall of civilizations, the difference in religions, the rise of science, the fascination of history. She continued her study of French—mainly because she wanted to know what Sara and Gabriel spoke about that they didn't want her to hear—and she sweated first-year biology. But by and large, she did well in her classes.

All too soon, final exams arrived. She sat in the library with other students, she and Darla trying to absorb what they needed to know to pass their courses. She'd already lived in the biology lab for several days after school with a study group, going over material that was certainly going to come up when they were tested.

"I'm going to fail," she moaned softly to Darla. "I'll go home in disgrace. I'll have to hide my head in a paper sack…."

"Shut up," Darla muttered. "You're going to pass! So am I. Be quiet and study, girl!"

Michelle sighed. "Thanks. I needed that."

"I'm going to fail," one of the boys nearby moaned to Darla. "I'll go home in disgrace…"

She punched him.

"Thanks." He chuckled, and went back to his books.

Michelle did pass, with flying colors, but she didn't know it when she went back to Comanche Wells for the holidays.

"I'll have to sweat it out until my grades come through," she said to Sara, hugging her warmly. "But I think I did okay." She looked past Sara and then at her, curious.

"He's out of the country," Sara said gently. "He was really sorry, he wanted to be home for the holidays. But it wasn't possible. This was a rush thing."

Michelle's heart fell. "I guess he has to work."

"Yes, he does. But he got your presents, and mine, and wrapped them before he left." Her dark eyes twinkled. "He promised that we'd love the gifts."

"I'd love a rock, if he picked it out for me," Michelle sighed. "Can we go shopping? Minette said I could work for her over the holidays while I'm home, so I'll have a little money of my own."

"Whenever you like, dear," Sara promised.

"Thanks!"

"Now come and have hot chocolate. I want to hear all about college!"

Minette had some interesting assignments for Michelle. One was to interview one of Jacobsville's senior citizens about Christmas celebrations in the mid-twentieth century, before the internet or space travel. It had sounded rather boring, honestly. But when she spoke to Adelaide Duncan, the old woman made the past come alive in her soft, mellow tones.

"We didn't have fancy decorations for the Christmas tree," Mrs. Duncan recalled, her pale blue eyes dancing with delightful memories. "We made them from construction paper. We made garlands of cranberries. We used candles set on the branches to light the tree, and we used soap powder mixed with a little water for snow. Presents were practical things, mostly fruit or nuts or handcrafted garments. One year I got oranges and a knit cap. Another, I got a dress my mother had made me in a beautiful lemon color. My husband kissed me under the mistletoe when we were still in school together, long before we married." Her face was wistful. "He was seventeen and I was fifteen. We danced to music that our parents and relatives made with fiddles and guitars. I wore the lemon-yellow dress, ruffled and laced, and I felt like I had possession of the whole world's treasures." She sighed. "We were married for fifty-five years," she added wistfully. "And one day, not too long away now, I'll see him again. And we'll dance together...."

Michelle had to fight tears. "Fifty-five years," she repeated, and couldn't imagine two people staying together for so long.

"Oh, yes. In my day, people got married and then had children." She shook her head. "The world has changed, my dear. Marriage doesn't seem to mean the same as it used to. History tends to repeat itself, and I fear when the stability of a civilization is lost, society crumbles. You'll study the results in your history classes in college," she added, nodding. "Do you have Dr. Barlane for history by any chance?"

"Yes," Michelle said, stunned.

The old woman laughed. "He and I graduated together from Marist College, both with degrees in history. But he went on to higher education and I got married and had a family. By and large, I think my life was happier than his. He never married."

"Do your children live here?" she asked.

"Oh, no, they're scattered around the world." She laughed. "I visit with them on Skype and we text back and forth every day, though. Modern technology." She shook her head. "It really is a blessing, in this day and time."

Michelle was surprised. "You text?" she asked.

"My dear," the old lady mused, laughing, "I not only text, I tweet and surf, and I am hell on wheels with a two-handed sword in World of Warcraft. I own a guild."

The younger woman's idea of elderly people had gone up in a blaze of disbelief. "You...play video games?"

"I eat them up." She shrugged. "I can't run and jump and play in real life, but I can do it online." She grinned from ear to ear. "Don't you dare tell Wofford Patterson, but I creamed one of his Horde toons last night on a battleground."

Michelle almost fell over laughing.

"And you thought you were going to interview some dried up old hulk who sat in a rocking chair and knitted, I bet," the woman mused with twinkling eyes.

"Yes, I did," Michelle confessed, "and I am most heartily sorry!"

"That's all right, dear," Mrs. Duncan said, patting her hand. "We all have misconceptions about each other."

"Mine were totally wrong."

"How nice of you to say so!"

Michelle changed gears and went back to the interview. But what she learned about elderly people that day colored her view of them forever.

"She plays video games," Michelle enthused to Minette, back at the office. She'd written her story and turned it in, along with her photos, while Minette was out of the office. Now she was elaborating on the story, fascinated with what she'd learned.

"Yes, there have been a lot of changes in the way we perceive the elderly," Minette agreed. "I live with my great-aunt. She doesn't play video games, but I did catch her doing Tai Chi along with an instructor on public television. And she can text, too."

"My grandparents sat and rocked on the porch after supper," Michelle recalled. "He smoked a pipe and she sewed quilt tops and they talked." She shook her head. "It's a different world."

"It is." She hesitated. "Has Gabriel come home?"

Michelle shook her head. "It's almost Christmas, too. We don't know where he is, or what he's doing."

Minette, who did, carefully concealed her knowledge.

"Well, he might surprise you and show up on Christmas day. Who knows?"

Michelle forced a smile. "Yes."

She and Sara decorated the tree. Two of the men who worked for Gabriel part-time, taking care of the horses and the ranch, had come in earlier with a big bucket, holding a tree with the root ball still attached.

"I can't bear to kill a tree," Sara confided as the men struggled to put it in place in the living room. "Sorry, guys," she added.

"Oh, Miss Sara, it's no trouble at all," the taller of the two cowboys said at once, holding his hat to his heart. He grinned. "It was our pleasure."

"Absolutely," the shorter one agreed.

They stood smiling at Sara until one thumped the other and reminded him that they had chores to do. They excused themselves, still smiling.

"You just tie them up in knots." Michelle laughed, when they were out of the room. "You're so pretty."

Sara made a face. "Nonsense."

"Hide your head in the sand, then. What are we going to decorate it with?" she added.

"Come with me."

Sara pulled down the ladder and the two women climbed carefully up into the attic.

Michelle caught her breath when she saw the heart of pine rafters. "My goodness, it's almost a religious experience to just look at them!" she exclaimed. "Those rafters must be a hundred years old!"

Sara glanced at her with amusement. "I believe they are. Imagine you, enthralled by rafters!"

"Heart of pine rafters," she replied. "My grandfather built houses when he was younger. He took me with him a time or two when he had to patch a roof or fix a leak. He was passionate about rafters." She laughed. "And especially those made of heart of pine. They're rare, these days, when people mostly build with green lumber that hasn't been properly seasoned."

"This house has a history," Sara said. "You probably already know it, since your people came from Jacobs County."

Michelle nodded, watching Sara pick up two boxes of ornaments and stack them together. "It belonged to a Texas Ranger."

"Yes. He was killed in a shoot-out in San Antonio. He left behind two sons, a daughter and a wife. There's a plaque in city hall in Jacobsville that tells all about him."

"I'll have to go look," Michelle said. "I haven't done any stories that took me there, yet."

"I'm sure you will. Minette says you're turning into a very good reporter."

"She does?" Michelle was all eyes. "Really?"

Sara looked at her and smiled. "You must have more confidence in yourself," she said gently. "You must believe in your own abilities."

"That's hard."

"It comes with age. You'll get the hang of it." She handed Michelle a box of ornaments. "Be careful going down the steps."

"Okay."

They spent the afternoon decorating the tree. When they finally plugged in the beautiful, colored fairy lights, Michelle caught her breath.

"It's the most breathtaking tree I've ever seen," she enthused.

"It is lovely, isn't it?" Sara asked. She fingered a

branch. "We must keep it watered, so that it doesn't die. When Christmas is over, I'll have the men plant it near the front steps. I do so love white pines!"

"Do you ever miss Wyoming?" Michelle asked, a little worried because she knew Sara was only here so that Michelle could come home, so that she wouldn't be alone with Gabriel.

Sara turned to her. "A little. I lived there because Gabriel bought the ranch and one of us needed to run it. But I had no real friends. I'm happier here." Her dark eyes were soft. She smoothed over an ornament. "This belonged to my grandmother," she said softly. It was a little house, made of logs, hanging from a red silk ribbon. "My grandfather whittled it for her, when they were dating." She laughed. "Wherever I am, it always makes me feel at home when the holidays come."

"Your mother's parents?"

Sara's face went hard. "No. My father's."

"I'm sorry."

Sara turned back to her. In her lovely face, her dark eyes were sad. "I don't speak of my mother, or her people. I'm sorry. It's a sore spot with me."

"I'll remember," Michelle said quietly. "It's like my stepmother."

"Exactly."

Michelle didn't betray her secret knowledge of Sara's early life, of the tragedy she and Gabriel had lived through because of their mother's passion for their stepfather. She changed the subject and asked about the other ornaments that Sara had placed on the tree.

But Sara wasn't fooled. She was very quiet. Later, when they were sipping hot chocolate in the kitchen, her dark eyes pinned Michelle.

"How much did he tell you?" she asked suddenly.

In her hands, the mug jumped, almost enough to spill the hot liquid on her fingers.

"Careful, it's hot," Sara said. "Come on, Michelle. How much did Gabriel tell you?"

Michelle grimaced.

Sara took in a long breath. "I see." She sipped the liquid gingerly. "He never speaks of it at all. Yet he told you." Her soft eyes lifted to Michelle's worried gray ones. "I'm not angry. I'm surprised."

"That he told me?"

"Yes." She smiled sadly. "He doesn't warm to people. In fact, he's cold and withdrawn with almost everyone. You can't imagine how shocked I was when he phoned me and asked me to come down here because of a young girl he was going to get custody of." She laughed, shaking her head. "I thought he was joking."

"But he's not. Cold and withdrawn, I mean." Michelle faltered.

"Not with you." She stared into Michelle's eyes earnestly. "I haven't heard Gabriel laugh in years," she added softly. "But he does it all the time with you. I don't understand it. But you give him peace, Michelle."

"That would be nice, if it were true. I don't know if it is," Michelle replied.

"It's fairly obvious what you feel for him."

She flushed. She couldn't lift her eyes.

"He won't take advantage of it, don't worry," Sara added gently. "That's why I'm here." She laughed. "He's taking no chances."

"He doesn't want to get involved with a child," Michelle said heavily.

"You won't be a child for much longer," the other woman pointed out.

"I'm sure he meets beautiful women all the time," Michelle said.

"I'm sure it doesn't matter what they look like," Sara replied. She smiled. "You'll see."

Michelle didn't reply to that. She just sipped her hot chocolate and felt warm inside.

It was the week before Christmas, a Friday about lunchtime, when the women heard a truck pull up in the driveway.

Michelle, who was petting one of the horses in the corral, saw the truck and gasped and ran as fast as she could to the man getting out of it.

"Gabriel!" she cried.

He turned. His face lit up like floodlights. He held out his arms and waited until she ran into them to pick her up and whirl her around, holding her so close that she felt they were going to be joined together forever.

"Oh, I've missed you," she choked.

"I've missed you." His voice was deep at her ear. He lifted his head and set her on her feet. His black eyes were narrow, intent on her face. He touched her mouth with just the tip of his forefinger, teasing it apart. His eyes fell to it and lingered there while her heart threatened to jump right out of her throat.

"Ma belle," he whispered roughly.

He framed her oval face in his big hands and searched her eyes. *"Ma belle,"* he repeated. His eyes fell to her mouth. "It's like falling into fire…"

As he spoke, his head started to bend. Michelle's heart ran away. She could hear her own breathing, feel his breath going into her mouth, taste the coffee and the faint odor of tobacco that came from him, mingled with some masculine cologne that teased her senses.

"Gabriel," she whispered, hanging at his mouth, aching to feel it come crashing down on her lips, crushing them, devouring him, easing the ache, the hunger that pulsed through her young, untried body...

"Gabriel!"

Sara's joyful cry broke them apart just in the nick of time. Gabriel cleared his throat, turned to his sister and hugged her.

"It's good to have you home," Sara said against his chest.

"It's good to be home." He was struggling to sound normal. His mind was still on Michelle's soft mouth and his hunger to break it open under his lips, back her into a wall and devour her.

"Have you eaten? I just made soup," Sara added.

"No. I'm starved." He made an attempt not to look at Michelle when he said that. He even smiled.

"I could eat, too," Michelle said, trying to break the tension.

"Let's go in." Sara took his arm. "Where did you come from?"

"Dallas, this time," he said. "I've been in the States for a couple of days, but I had business there before I could get home." He hesitated. "I got tickets to the ballet in San Antonio when I came through there this morning." He glanced at Michelle. "Want to go see *The Nutcracker* with me?" he added with a grin.

"Oh, I'd love to," she said fervently. "What do we wear?"

"A very dressy evening outfit," Sara said. "I bought you one once, and you never even wore it."

Michelle grinned. "Well, I haven't been anywhere I'd need to wear it," she replied, not guessing what it told Gabriel, whose eyes twinkled brightly.

Michelle flushed and then grinned at him. "No, I'm not dating anybody at college," she said. She shrugged. "I'm too busy studying."

"Is that so?" Gabriel laughed, and was relieved.

"When are you leaving?" Sara asked.

"At six, and you'd better start dressing as well, because we're all three going," Gabriel added, and he exchanged a speaking look with Sara.

"All of us? Oh. Oh! That's nice!" Michelle worked at sounding enthusiastic.

Sara just winked at her. "I'd better go through my closet."

Gabriel looked down at Michelle with the Christmas tree bright and beautiful behind her. "I wouldn't dare take you out alone, *ma belle,*" he said under his breath. "You know it. And you know why."

Her eyes searched his hungrily. She knew. She'd felt it, when he held her beside the truck. She knew that he wanted her.

She'd had no idea what wanting really was, until Gabriel had come into her life. Now she was aware of a hunger that came around when he was close, that grew and surged in her when he looked at her, when he spoke to her, when he touched her....

"Yes, you know, don't you?" he breathed, standing a little too close. He rubbed his thumb against her lips, hard enough to make her gasp and shiver with delight. His black eyes narrowed. "It's too soon. You know that, too."

She ground her teeth together as she looked at him. He was the most perfect thing in her life. He was preaching caution when all she wanted to do was push him down on the floor and spread her body over him and...

She didn't know what would come next. She'd read books, but they were horribly lacking in preliminaries.

"What are you thinking about so hard?" he asked.

"About pushing you down on the floor," she blurted out, and flushed. "But I don't know what comes next, exactly…"

He burst out laughing.

"You stop that," she muttered. "I'll bet you weren't born knowing what to do, either."

"I wasn't," he confessed. He touched her nose with the tip of his finger. "It's just as well that you don't know. Yet. And we aren't going to be alone. Yet."

She drew in a long sigh and smiled. "Okay."

He chuckled.

"I've never been to the ballet," she confessed.

"High time you went," he replied, and he laughed. "Go on."

Sara had laid out the most beautiful black velvet dress Michelle had ever seen. It had a discreet rounded neckline and long sleeves, and it fell to the ankles, with only a slight tuck where the waistline was.

"It's gorgeous!" Michelle enthused.

"And you'll look gorgeous in it," Sara replied. She hugged Michelle. "It's yours. I have shoes and a purse to match it."

"But, I have a dress," Michelle began.

"A summer dress," Sara said patiently, and smiled. "This one is more suitable for winter. I have one similar to it that I'm wearing. We'll look like twins." She grinned.

"Okay, then. And thank you!" Michelle said heartily.

"You're very welcome."

Chapter Ten

Gabriel wore a dress jacket with dark slacks and a black turtleneck sweater. He looked classy and elegant. Sara wore a simple sheath of navy blue velvet with an expensive gold necklace and earrings and looked exquisite, with her silky black hair loose almost to her waist and her big, dark eyes soft in her beautiful face.

Michelle in her black velvet dress felt like royalty. The trio drew eyes as they filed into the auditorium where the ballet was being performed.

Up front, in the orchestra pit, the musicians were tuning up their instruments. Gabriel found their seats and let the women go in first before he took his place on the aisle.

"There's quite a crowd," Michelle remarked as more people filed in.

"Oh, dear." Sara's voice was full of consternation.

Before Michelle could ask what was wrong, she saw it for herself. Wofford Patterson, in a dinner jacket with a white tie and black slacks was escorting a beautiful blonde, in an elegant green velvet gown, down the aisle—directly to the seats beside Sara.

"Mr. Brandon," Wolf said, nodding. "This is Elise Jorgansen. Elise, Gabriel Brandon. That's his sister, Sara. And that's his ward, Michelle."

"Nice to meet you," Elise said, and smiled at them all with genuine warmth.

"I believe our seats are right there," Wolf told the pretty woman. He escorted her past Gabriel and the women with apologies, because it was a tight squeeze. He sat next to Sara, with Elise on his other side.

Sara tensed and glared straight ahead. Wolf grinned.

"I didn't know that you liked the ballet, Miss Brandon," Wolf said politely.

"I like this one. It's *The Nutcracker,*" she added with a venomous look at the man beside her.

He pursed his lips. "Left the flying monkeys at home, did we?"

"I'd love to drop a house on you, dear man," she said under her breath.

"Now, now, it's the ballet," he pointed out. "We must behave like civilized people."

"You'd need so much instruction for that, Mr. Patterson," Sara said, her voice dripping honey.

"Isn't the music lovely?" Michelle broke in.

The music was the instruments being tuned, but it shattered the tension and everyone laughed.

"Behave," Gabriel whispered to his sister.

She gave him an irritated look, but she kept her hands in her lap and sat quietly as the ballerinas came onstage one by one and the performance began, to Michelle's utter fascination and delight. She'd never seen a live performance of the ballet, which was her favorite.

At intermission, Sara excused herself and left the row.

"I'm not getting up," Wolf said. "I'd never get back in here."

"Neither am I," Gabriel mused. "It's quite a crowd."

"You seem to be enjoying the music, Miss Godfrey," Wolf said politely.

"I've never been to a ballet before," she replied, laughing. "It's so beautiful!"

"You should see it in New York City, at the American Ballet Company," Gabriel said gently.

"They do an excellent performance," Wolf agreed. "Have you seen it at the Bolshoi?" he added.

"Yes," Gabriel agreed. "Theirs is unbelievably beautiful."

"That's in Russia, isn't it?" Michelle asked, wide-eyed.

"Yes," Gabriel said. He smiled down at her. "One day, Sara and I will have to take you traveling."

"You should see the world," Elise agreed, from beside Wolf. "Or at least, some of it. Travel broadens your world."

"I can't think of anything I'd love more," Michelle replied, smiling back at the woman.

"Elise studied ballet when she was still in school," Wolf said. "She was in line to be a prima ballerina with the company she played with in New York."

"Don't," Elise said gently.

"Sorry," Wolf said, patting her hand. "Bad memories. I won't mention it again."

"That life is long over," she replied. "But I still love going to see the ballet and the theater and opera. We have such a rich cultural heritage here in San Antonio."

"We do, indeed," Gabriel agreed.

The musicians began tuning their instruments again,

just as Sara came back down the aisle, so graceful and poised that she drew male eyes all the way.

"Your sister has an elegance of carriage that is quite rare," Elise said to Gabriel as she approached.

"She also studied ballet," Gabriel replied quietly. "But the stress of dancing and trying to get through college became too much. She gave up ballet and got her degree in languages." He laughed. "She still dances, though," he added. "She just doesn't put on a tutu first."

"It wouldn't go with the broom," Sara said to Wolf, and smiled coldly as she sat down.

"Broom?" Elise asked, curious.

"Never mind. I'll explain it to you later," Wolf replied.

Sara gave him a look that might have curdled milk and turned her attention to the stage as the curtain began to rise.

"Well, it was a wonderful evening," Michelle said dreamily as she followed them out to the car. "Thank you so much for taking us," she added to Gabriel.

He studied her in the lovely dress, smiling. "It was my pleasure. We'll have to do this more often."

"Expose you to culture, he means," Sara said in a stage whisper. "It's good for you."

"I really had a good time."

"I would have, except for the company," Sara muttered. She flushed. "Not you two," she said hastily when they gaped at her. "That…man! And his date."

"I thought Elise was very nice," Michelle ventured.

Sara clammed up.

Gabriel just chuckled.

Christmas Eve was magical. They sat around the Christmas tree, watching a program of Christmas music on television, sipping hot chocolate and making s'mores in the fireplace, where a sleepy fire flamed every now and then.

In all her life, Michelle couldn't remember being so happy. Her eyes kept darting to Gabriel, when she thought he wasn't looking. Even in jeans and a flannel shirt, he was the stuff of dreams. It was so hard not to appear starstruck.

They opened presents that night instead of the next morning, because Sara announced that she wasn't getting up at dawn to see what Santa had left.

She gave Michelle a beautiful scarf of many colors, a designer one. Michelle draped it around her neck and raved over it. Then she opened Gabriel's gift. It was pearls, a soft off-white set in a red leather box. They were Japanese. He'd brought them home from his last trip and hidden them to give at Christmas. The necklace was accompanied by matching drop earrings.

"I was right," he mused as Michelle tried them on enthusiastically. "They're just the right shade."

"They are, indeed. And thank you for mine, also, my sweet." Sara kissed his tan cheek, holding a strand of white ones in her hand. They suited her delicate coloring just as the off-white ones suited Michelle's.

"I like mine, too." He held up a collection of DVDs of shows he particularly liked from Michelle and a black designer turtleneck from Sara.

Sara loved her handmade scarf from Michelle. It was crocheted and had taken an age to finish. It was the softest white knit, with tassels. "I'll wear it all winter," she promised Michelle, and kissed her, too.

Michelle had hung mistletoe in strategic places, but she hadn't counted on Gabriel's determined reticence. He kissed her on the cheek, smiled and wished her the happiest of Christmases and New Years. She pretended that it didn't matter that he didn't drag her into an empty room and kiss her half to death. He was determined not to treat her as an adult. It was painful. But in some sense, she did understand.

So three years went by, more quickly than Michelle had dreamed they would. She got a job part-time with a daily newspaper in San Antonio and did political pieces for it while she got through her core courses and into serious journalism in college.

She went to class during summer to speed up her degree program, although she came home for the holidays. Gabriel was almost always away now. Sara was there, although she spent most of her time in Wyoming at the ranch she and Gabriel owned. Michelle had gone up there with her one summer for a couple of weeks during her vacation. It was a beautiful place. Sara was different somehow. Something had happened between her and Wofford Patterson. She wouldn't talk about it, but she knew that it had changed Sara. Gabriel had mentioned something about Sara going back into therapy and there had been an argument in French that Michelle couldn't follow.

Wofford Patterson had also moved up to Catelow, Wyoming. He bought a huge ranch there near Sara's. He kept his place in Comanche Wells, but he put in a foreman to manage it for him. He had business interests in Wyoming that took up much of his time, he said, and it was hard to commute. Sara didn't admit that she was glad to have him as a neighbor. But Michelle suspected that she did.

Sara was still playing her online game with her friend, and they fought battles together late into the night. She still didn't know who he really was, either. Gabriel had made sure of it.

"He's such a gentleman," Sara mused over coffee one morning, her face bright with pleasure. "He wants to meet me in person." She hesitated. "I'm not sure about that."

"Why not, if you like him?" Michelle asked innocently, although she didn't dare let on that she knew exactly who Sara's friend was, and she knew that Sara would have a stroke if she saw him in person. It would be the end of a lovely online relationship.

"People aren't what they seem," Sara replied, and pain was in her eyes. "If it seems too good to be true, it usually is."

"He might be a knight in shining armor," Michelle teased. "You should find out."

"He might be an ogre who lives in a cave with bats, too." Sara chuckled. "No. I like things the way they are. I really don't want to try to have a relationship with a man in real life." Her face tensed. "I never wanted to."

Michelle grimaced. "Sara, you're so beautiful…"

"Beautiful!" She laughed coldly. "I wish I'd been born ugly. It would have made my life so much easier. You don't know…" She drew in a harsh breath. "Well, actually, you do know." She managed a soft smile. "We're all prisoners of our childhoods, Michelle. Mine was particularly horrible. It warped me."

"You should have been in therapy," Michelle said gently.

"I tried therapy. It only made things worse. I can't talk to total strangers."

"Maybe you just talked to the wrong person."

Sara's eyes were suddenly soft and dreamy and she flushed. "I think I did. So much has changed," she added softly.

Michelle, who had a good idea what was going on up in Wyoming, just grinned.

Sara's eyes took on an odd, shimmering softness. "Life is so much sweeter than I dreamed it could be." She smiled to herself and looked at her watch. "I have some phone calls to make. I love having you around." She added, "Thanks."

"For what?"

"For caring," Sara said simply.

Michelle was looking forward to her last Christmas in college. She got talked into a blind date with Darla's boyfriend's friend. He turned out to be a slightly haughty man who worked as a stockbroker and never stopped talking on his cell phone for five seconds. He was at it all through dinner. Bob, Darla's boyfriend, looked very uncomfortable and apologetic.

"Bob feels awful," Darla whispered to Michelle in the restroom after they'd finished eating. "Larry seemed to be a normal guy."

"He just lives and breathes his job. Besides," she added, "you know there's only one man who interests me at all. And it's never going to be someone like Larry."

"Having seen your Mr. Brandon, I totally understand." Darla giggled. She shook her head. "He is a dreamboat."

"I think so."

"Well, we'll stop by the bar for a nightcap and go home. Maybe we can pry Larry away from his phone long enough to say good-night."

"I wish I was riding with you and Bob," Michelle sighed. "At least he stops talking while he's driving."

"Curious, that he didn't want to ride with Bob," Darla said. "Well, that's just men, I guess."

But Larry had an agenda that the girls weren't aware of. He knew that Bob and Darla were going dancing and wouldn't be home soon. So when he walked Michelle to the door of the apartment she and Darla shared, he pushed his way in and took off his jacket.

"Finally, alone together," he enthused, and reached for her. "Now, sweetie, let's have a little payback for the meal and the drinks…"

"Are you out of your mind?" she gasped, avoiding his grasping arms.

"I paid for the food," he said, almost snarling. "You owe me!"

"I owe you? Like hell I owe you!" She got to the door and opened it. "I'll send you a check for my part of the meal! Get out!"

"I'm not leaving. You just want to play hard to get." He started to push the door closed. And connected with a steely big hand that caught him by the arm, turned him around and booted him out into the night.

"Gabriel!" Michelle gasped.

"You can't do that to me…!" Larry said angrily, getting to his feet.

Gabriel fell into a fighting stance. "Come on," he said softly. "I could use the exercise."

Larry came to his senses. He glanced at Michelle. She went back inside, got his jacket, and threw it at him.

"Dinner doesn't come with bed," she told him icily.

Larry started to make a reply, but Gabriel's expression was a little too unsettling. He muttered something under his breath, turned, slammed into his car and roared away.

Gabriel went inside with Michelle, who was tearing up now that the drama had played itself out.

"Ah, no, *ma belle*," he whispered. "There's no need for tears." He pulled her into his arms, bent his head, and kissed her so hungrily that she forgot to breathe.

He lifted his head. His black eyes were smoldering, so

full of desire that they mesmerized Michelle. She tasted him on her mouth, felt the heavy throb of his heart under her hands.

"Finally," he breathed, pulling her close. He brushed his lips over her soft mouth. "Finally!"

She opened her mouth to ask what he meant, and the kiss knocked her so off balance that she couldn't manage a single word in reply. She held on with all her might, clung to him, pushed her body into his so that she could feel every movement of his powerful body against her. He was aroused, very quickly, and even that didn't intimidate her. She moaned. Which only made matters worse.

He picked her up, still kissing her, and laid her out on the couch, easing his body down over hers in a silence that throbbed with frustrated desire.

"Soft," he whispered. "Soft and sweet. All mine."

She would have said something, but he was kissing her again, and she couldn't think at all. She felt his big, rough hands go under her dress, up and up, touching and exploring, testing softness, finding her breasts under the lacy little bra.

"You feel like silk all over," he murmured. He found the zipper and eased her out of the dress and the half slip under it, then out of the bra, so that all she had left on were her briefs. He kissed his way down her body, lingering on her pert breasts with their tight little crowns, savoring her soft, helpless cries of pleasure.

It excited him to know that she'd never done this. He ate her up like candy, tasting her hungrily. He nuzzled her breasts, kissing their soft contours with a practiced touch that made her rise up in an aching arch to his lips.

Somehow, his jacket and shirt ended up on the floor. She felt the rough, curling hair on his chest against her bare breasts as his body covered hers. His powerful legs eased between her own, so that she could feel with him an intimacy she'd never shared with anyone.

She cried out as he moved against her. Sensations were piling on each other, dragging her under, drowning her in pleasure. She clung to him, pleading for more, not even knowing exactly what she wanted, but so drawn with tension that she was dying for it to ease.

She felt hot tears run down her cheeks as his mouth moved back onto hers. He touched her as he never had before. She shivered. The touch came again. She sobbed, and opened her mouth under his. She felt his tongue go into her mouth, as his hands moved on her more intimately.

Suddenly, like a fall of fire, a flash of agonized pleasure convulsed the soft body under his. He groaned and had to fight the instinctive urge to finish what he started, to go right into her, push inside her, take what was his, what had always been his.

But she was a virgin. His exploration had already told him that. He'd known already, by her reactions. She was very much a virgin. He didn't want to do this. Not yet. She was his. It must be done properly, in order, in a way that wouldn't shame her to remember somewhere down the line.

So he forced his shivering body to bear the pain. He held her very close while she recovered from her first ecstasy. He wrapped her up tight, and held her while he endured what he must to spare her innocence.

She wept. He kissed away the tears, so tenderly that they fell even harder, hot and wet on her flushed cheeks.

She was embarrassed and trying not to let him see.

He knew. He smiled and kissed her eyes shut. "It had to be with me," he whispered. "Only with me. I would rather die than know you had such an experience with any other man."

She opened her eyes and looked up into his. "Really?"

"Really." He looked down at her nudity, his eyes hungry again at the sight of her pink-and-peach skin, silky and soft and fragrant. He touched her breasts tenderly. "You are the most beautiful woman I will ever see."

Her lips parted on a shaky breath.

He bent and kissed her breasts. "And now we have to get up."

She stared at him.

"Or not get up," he murmured with a laugh. "Because I can't continue this much longer."

"It would be…all right," she whispered. "If you wanted to," she added.

"I want to," he said huskily. "But you won't be happy afterward. And you know it. Not like this, *ma belle*. Not our first time together. It has to be done properly."

"Properly?"

"You graduate from college, get a job, go to work. I come to see you bringing flowers and chocolates," he mused, tracing her mouth. "And then, eventually, a ring."

"A ring."

He nodded.

"An…engagement…ring?"

He smiled.

"People do it all the time, even before they get engaged," she said.

He got to his feet. "They do. But we won't."

"Oh."

He dressed her, enjoying the act of putting back onto her lovely body the things he'd taken off it. He laughed at her rapt expression. "You have a belief system that isn't going to allow a more modern approach to sex," he said blandly. "So we do it your way."

"I could adjust," she began, still hungry.

"Your happiness means a lot to me," he said simply. "I'm not going to spoil something beautiful with a tarnished memory. Not after I've waited so long."

She stared up into his black eyes. "I've waited for you, too," she whispered.

"I know." He smoothed back her hair just as they heard a car door slam and footsteps approaching.

Michelle looked horrified, thinking what could have happened, what condition they could have been in as Darla put her key into the lock.

Gabriel burst out laughing at her expression. "Now was I right?" he asked.

The door opened. Darla stopped with Bob in tow and just stared at Gabriel. Then she grinned. "Wow," she said. "Look what Larry changed into!"

And they all burst out laughing.

Michelle graduated with honors. Gabriel and Sara were both there for the ceremony, applauding when she walked down the aisle to accept her diploma. They went out to eat afterward, but once they were home, Gabriel couldn't stay. He was preoccupied, and very worried, from the look of things.

"Can you tell me what's wrong?" Michelle asked.

He shook his head. He bent to kiss her, very gently. "I'm going to have to be out of the country for two or three months."

"No!" she exclaimed.

"Only that. Then I have a job waiting, one that won't require so much travel," he promised. "Bear with me. I'm sorry. I have to do this."

She drew in a long breath. "Okay. If you have to go."

"You've got a job waiting in San Antonio, anyway," he reminded her with a smile. "On a daily newspaper. It has a solid reputation for reporting excellence. Make a name for yourself. But don't get too comfortable there," he added enigmatically. "Because when I get back, we need to talk."

"Talk." She smiled.

"And other things."

"Oh, yes, especially, other things," she whispered, dragging his mouth down to hers. She kissed him hungrily. He returned the kiss, but drew back discreetly when Sara came into the room. He hugged her, too.

He paused in the doorway and looked back at them, smiling. "Take care of each other." He grinned at his sister. "Happy?" he asked, referring to the changes in her life.

Sara laughed, tossing her long hair. "I could die of it," she sighed.

"I'll be back before you miss me," he told Michelle, who was looking sad. He wanted to kiss her, right there in front of the world. But it wasn't the time. And he wasn't sure he could stop.

"Impossible," Michelle said softly. "I miss you already."

He winked and closed the door.

Michelle liked the job. She had a desk and three years of solid education behind her to handle the assignments she was given.

A big story broke the second month she'd been with the newspaper. There was a massacre of women and children in a small Middle Eastern nation, perpetrated, it was said, by a group of mercenaries led by a Canadian national named Angel Le Veut. He had ties to an anti-terrorism school run by a man named Eb Scott in, of all places, Jacobsville, Texas.

Michelle went on the offensive at once, digging up everything she could find about the men in the group who had killed the women and children in the small Muslim community that was at odds with a multinational occupation force.

The name of the man accused of leading the assault was ironic. One of the languages she'd studied was French. And if loosely translated, the man's name came out as "Angel wants it." It was an odd play on words that was used most notably in the sixteenth century by authorities when certain cases were tried and a guilty verdict was desired. The phrase *"Le Roi le Veut"* meant that the king wanted the accused found guilty—whether or not he really was, apparently. The mysterious Angel was obviously an educated man with a knowledge of European history. Michelle was puzzled over why such a man would choose a lifestyle that involved violence.

Her first stop was Jacobsville, Texas, where she arranged an interview with Eb Scott, the counterterrorism expert, whose men had been involved in the massacre. Michelle knew him, from a distance.

Her father had gone to school with him and they were acquaintances. Her father had said there wasn't a finer man anywhere, that Eb was notorious for backing lost causes and fighting for the underdog. That didn't sound like a man who would order the murder of helpless women and children.

Eb shook her hand and invited her into his house. His wife and children were gone for the day, shopping in San Antonio for summer clothing. It was late spring already.

"Thank you for seeing me," Michelle said when they were seated. "Especially under the circumstances."

"Hiding from the press is never a good idea, but at times, in matters like this, it's necessary, until the truth can be ferreted out," Eb said solemnly. His green eyes searched hers. "You're Alan Godfrey's daughter."

"Yes," she said, smiling.

"You used to spend summers in Comanche Wells with your grandparents." He smiled back. "Minette Carson speaks well of you. She did an interview with me yesterday. Hopefully, some of the truth will trickle down to the mass news media before they crucify my squad leader."

"Yes. This man, Angel," she began, looking over her notes while Eb Scott grimaced and tried not to reveal what he really knew about the man, "his name is quite odd."

"Le Veut?" He smiled again. "He gets his way. He's something of an authority on sixteenth-century European history. He and Kilraven, one of the feds who's married to a local girl, go toe-to-toe over whether or not Mary Queen of Scots really helped Lord Bothwell murder her husband."

"Has this man worked for you, with you, for a long time?" she asked.

He nodded. "Many years. He's risked his life time and time again to save innocents. I can promise you that when the truth comes out, and it will, he'll be exonerated."

She was typing on her small notebook computer as he spoke. "He's a Canadian national?"

"He has dual citizenship, here and in Canada," he corrected. "But he's lived in the States most of his life."

"Does he live in Jacobsville?"

Eb hesitated.

She lifted her hands from the keyboard. "You wouldn't

want to say, would you?" she asked perceptibly. "If he has family, it could hurt them, as well. There wouldn't be a place they could go where the media wouldn't find them."

"The media can be like a dog after a juicy bone," Eb said with some irritation. "They'll get fed one way or the other, with truth or, if time doesn't permit, with lies. I've seen lives ruined by eager reporters out to make a name for themselves." He paused. "Present company excepted," he added gently. "I know all about you from Minette."

She smiled gently. "Thanks. I always try to be fair and present both sides of the story without editorializing. I don't like a lot of what I see on television, presented as fair coverage. Most of the commentators seem quite biased to me. They convict people and act as judge, jury and executioner." She shook her head. "I like the paper I work for. Our editor, even our publisher, are fanatics for accurate and fair coverage. They fired a reporter last month whose story implicated an innocent man. He swore he had eyewitnesses to back up the facts, and that he could prove them. Later, when the editor sent other reporters out to recheck—after the innocent man's attorneys filed a lawsuit—they found that the reporter had ignored people who could verify the man's whereabouts at the time of the crime. The reporter didn't even question them."

Eb sighed, leaning back in his recliner. "That happens all too often. Even on major newspapers," he added, alluding to a reporter for one of the very large East Coast dailies who'd recently been let go for fabricating stories.

"We try," Michelle said quietly. "We really try. Most reporters only want to help people, to point out problems, to help better the world around us."

"I know that. It's the one bad apple in the barrel that pollutes the others," he said.

"This man, Angel, is there any way I could interview him?"

He almost bit through his lip. He couldn't tell her that. "No," he said finally. "We've hidden him in a luxury hotel in a foreign country. The news media will have a hell of a time trying to ferret him out. We have armed guards in native dress everywhere. Meanwhile, I've hired an investigative firm out of Houston—Dane Lassiter's—to dig out the truth. Believe me, there's no one in the world better at it. He's a former Houston policeman."

"I know of him," she replied. "His son was involved in a turf war between drug lords in the area, wasn't he?"

"Yes, he was. That was a while back."

"Well, tell me what you can," she said. "I'll do my best not to convict the man in print. The mercenaries who were with Angel," she added, "are they back in the States?"

"That's another thing I can't tell you right now," he replied. "I'm not trying to be evasive. I'm protecting my men from trial by media. We have attorneys for all of them, and our investigator hopes to have something concrete for us, and the press, very soon."

"That's fair enough."

"Here's what we know right now," Eb said. "My squad leader was given an assignment by a State Department official to interview a local tribesman in a village in Anasrah. The man had information about a group of terrorists who were hiding in the village—protected by a high-ranking government official, we were told. My squad leader, in disguise, took a small team in to interview him, but when he and his men arrived, the tribesman and his entire family were dead. One of the terrorists pointed the finger at Angel and accused his team of the atrocity. I'm certain the terrorist was paid handsomely to do it."

Michelle frowned. "You believe that?"

Eb stared her down with glittering green eyes. "Miss Godfrey, if you knew Angel, you wouldn't have to ask me that question."

"Sorry," she said. "It's my job, Mr. Scott."

He let out a breath. "You can't imagine how painful this is for me," he said. "Men I trained, men I've worked with, accused of something so inhuman." His face hardened. "Follow the money. It's all about the money, I assure you," he added curtly. "Someone stands to lose a lot of it if the truth comes out."

"I can only imagine how bad it must be," she said, and not without sympathy.

She asked questions, he answered them. She was impressed by him. He wasn't at all the sort of person that she'd pictured when she heard people speak of mercenaries. Even the word meant a soldier for hire, a man who sold his talents to the highest bidder. But Eb Scott's organization trained men in counterterrorism. He had an enormous operation in Jacobsville, and men and women came from around the world to learn from his experts. There were rumors that a few government agents had also availed themselves of his expertise.

The camp was state-of-the-art, with every electronic gadget known to modern science—and a few things that were largely experimental. They taught everything from evasive driving techniques to disarming bombs, improvised weapons, stealth, martial arts, the works. Michelle was allowed to photograph only a small section of the entire operation, and she wasn't allowed to photograph any of his instructors or the students. But even with the reservations on what she was shown, what she learned fascinated her.

"Well, I'll never think of mercenaries the same way

again, Mr. Scott," she said when she was ready to leave. "This operation is very impressive."

"I'm glad you think so."

She paused at the door and turned. "You know, the electronic media have resources that those of us in print journalism don't. I mean, we have a digital version of our paper online, like most everyone does. But the big networks employ dozens of experts who can find out anything. If they want to find your man, they will. And his family."

"Miss Godfrey, for the sake of a lot of innocent people, I hope you're wrong."

The way he said it stayed on her mind for hours after she left.

Chapter Eleven

Michelle wrote the story, and she did try to be fair. But when she saw the photographs of the massacre, the bodies of small children with women and men weeping over them, her heart hardened. If the man was guilty, he should be hanged for this.

She didn't slant the story. She presented the facts from multiple points of view. She interviewed a man in Saudi Arabia who had a friend in Anasrah with whom he'd recently spoken. She interviewed a representative of the State Department, who said that one of their staff had been led into the village by a minor government official just after the attack and was adamant that the mercenaries had been responsible for the slaughter. She also interviewed an elder in the village, through an interpreter, who said that an American had led the attack.

There was another man, also local, who denied that a foreigner was responsible. He was shouted down by the others, but Michelle managed to get their representative in Saudi Arabia to go to Anasrah, a neighboring country, and interview the man in the village. His story contradicted the others. He said that it was a man well-known in terrorist circles who had come into the village and accused the tribesmen of betraying their own people by working with the government and foreigners. He said that if it continued, an example, a horrible example, would be made, he would see to it personally.

The local man said that he could prove that the terrorists themselves had perpetrated the attack, if he had time.

Michelle made the first big mistake of her career in journalism by discounting the still, small voice in the wilderness. The man's story didn't ring true. She took notes, and filed them on her computer. But when she wrote the story, she left out what sounded like a made-up tale.

The story broke with the force of bombs. All of a sudden, it was all anyone heard on the media. The massacre in Anasrah, the children murdered by foreigners, the mercenaries who had cut them down with automatic weapons while their parents pleaded for mercy. On television, the weeping relatives were interviewed. Their stories brought even hardened commentators to tears on-screen.

Michelle's story, with its unique point of view and Eb Scott's interview—which none of the national media had been able to get, because he refused to talk to them—put her in the limelight for the first time. Her story was reprinted partially in many national papers, and she was interviewed by the major news networks, as well. She respected Eb Scott, she added, and she thought he was sincere, but she wept for the dead children and she thought the mercenary responsible should be tried in the world court and imprisoned for the rest of his life.

Her impulsive comment was broadcast over and over. And just after that came the news that the mercenary had a sister, living in Wyoming. They had her name, as well. Sara.

It could have been a coincidence. Except that suddenly she remembered that the man, Angel, had both American and Canadian citizenship. Now she learned that he had a sister named Sara. Gabriel was gone for long periods of time overseas on jobs. Michelle still tried to persuade herself that it wasn't, couldn't, be Gabriel.

Until Sara called her on the phone.

"I couldn't believe it when they said you broke the story," she said in a cold tone. "How could you do this to us?"

"Sara, it wasn't about anyone you know," she said quickly. "It was about a mercenary who gunned down little children in a Middle Eastern village…!"

"He did nothing of the sort," Sara said, her voice dripping ice. "It was the tribesman's brother-in-law, one of the terrorists, who killed the man and his family and then blamed it on Angel and his men."

"Do you know this man Angel?" Michelle asked, a sick feeling in her stomach because Sara sounded so harsh.

"Know him." Her laugh was as cold as death. "We both know him, Michelle. He uses Angel as an alias when he goes on missions for Eb Scott's clients. But his name is Gabriel."

Michelle felt her blood run cold. Images flashed through her mind. Dead children. The one dissenting voice, insisting that it was the terrorists not the Americans who perpetrated the horror. Her refusal to listen, to print the other side of the story. Gabriel's side. She'd convinced herself that it couldn't be Gabriel. Now she had to face facts.

"I didn't know," she said, her voice breaking. "Sara, believe me, I didn't know!"

"Eb told you it wasn't him," Sara said furiously. "But you wouldn't listen. I had a contact in the State Department send a man to tell your newspaper's agent about the dead man's brother-in-law. And you decided not to print it. Didn't you? God forbid you should run against the voice of the world press and risk your own glowing reputation as a crusader for justice by dissenting!"

"I didn't know," Michelle repeated through tears.

"You didn't know! If Gabriel ends up headfirst in a ditch somewhere, it will be all right, because you didn't know! Would you like to see the road in front of our ranch here in Wyoming, Michelle?" she added. "It looks like a tent city, surrounded by satellite trucks. They're certain they'll wear me down and I'll come out and accuse my brother for them!"

"I'm so sorry." Michelle didn't have to be told that Gabriel was innocent. She knew he was. But she'd helped convict him.

"You're sorry. I'll be certain to tell him when, and if, I see him again." There was a harshly indrawn breath. "He phoned me two days ago," she said in a haunted voice. "They're hunting him like an animal, thanks to you. When I told him who sold him out, he wouldn't believe me. It wasn't until I sent him a link to your story that he saw for himself."

Michelle felt every drop of blood draining out of her face. "What...did he say?"

"He said," Sara replied, enunciating every word, "that he'd never been so wrong about anyone in his life. He thought that you, of all people, would defend him even against the whole world. He said," she added coldly, "that he never wanted to see you or hear from you again as long as he lived."

The words were like bullets. She could actually feel their impact.

"I loved you like my own sister," Sara said, her voice breaking. "And I will never, never forgive you!" She slammed down the phone.

Michelle realized after a minute that she hadn't broken the connection. She hung up her own telephone. She sat down heavily and heard the recriminations break over her head again and again.

She remembered Eb Scott's certainty that his man would never do such a thing. Sara's fierce anger. It had been easy to discount them while Angel was a shadowy figure without substance. But Michelle knew Gabriel. And she was certain, absolutely certain, that the man who'd saved her from suicide would never put another human being in harm's way.

It took two days for the effects of Sara's phone call to wear off enough that she could stop crying and blaming herself. The news media was having a field day with the story, running updates about it all day, every day, either in newscasts or in banners under the anchor people. Michelle finally had to turn off the television to escape it, so that she could get herself back together.

She wanted, so desperately, to make up for what she'd done. But she didn't even know where to start. The story was everywhere. People were condemning the American mercenaries on every news program in the world.

But Gabriel was innocent. Michelle had helped convict him in the press, without knowing who she was writing about. Now it was her turn to do her job properly, and give both sides of the story, however unpopular. She had to save him, if she could, even if he hated her forever for what she'd done.

So she went back to work. Her first act was to contact the newspaper's man in Saudi Arabia and ask him to repeat the story his informant in Anasrah had told him. Then she contacted Eb Scott and gave him the information, so that he could pass it on to his private investigator. Before she did that, she asked him to call her back on a secure line, because she knew how some of the tabloid news bureaus sometimes had less scrupulous agents digging out information.

"You're learning, Miss Godfrey," Eb said solemnly.

"Not soon enough. I know who Angel is now," she added heavily. "His sister hates me. He told her that he never wanted to see or speak to me again, either. And I deserve that. I wasn't objective, and people are paying for my error. But I have to do what I can to undo the mess I helped make. I'm sorry I didn't listen."

"Too little, and almost too late," he said brutally. "Learn from it. Sometimes the single dissenting voice is the right one."

"I won't forget," she said.

He hung up.

She tried to phone Sara back and apologize once again, to tell her she was trying to repair the damage. But Sara wouldn't accept the first phone call and after that, her number was blocked. She was heartsick. The Brandons had been so good to her. They'd made sacrifices to get her through school, through college, always been there when she needed help. And she'd repaid them like this. It wounded her as few things in life ever had.

When she tried to speak to her editor in confidence, to backtrack on the story she'd written, he laughed it off. The man was obviously guilty, he said, why make waves now? She'd made a name for herself in investigative reporting, it was all good.

She told him that Angel wasn't the sort of person to ever harm a child. Then he wanted to know how she knew that. She wouldn't reveal her source, she said, falling back on a tried and true response. But the man was innocent.

Her editor had just laughed. So she thought the guy was innocent, what did it matter? The news was the thing that mattered, scooping all the other media and being first and best at delivering the story. She'd given the facts of the matter, that was the end of it. She should just enjoy her celebrity status while it lasted.

Michelle went back to her apartment that night saddened and weary, with a new sense of disillusionment about life and people.

The next morning, she phoned Minette Carson and asked if she had an opening for a reporter who was certain she wasn't cut out for the big dailies.

Minette was hesitant.

"Look, never mind," Michelle said gently. "I know I've made a lot of enemies in Jacobsville with the way I covered the story. It's okay. I can always teach journalism. I'll be a natural at showing students what not to do."

"We all have to start somewhere when we learn how to do a job," Minette replied. "Usually, it's a painful process. Eb Scott called and asked me, before you did the interview, if you knew who Gabriel really was. I told him no. I knew you'd have said something long before this. I should have told you."

"I should have suspected something," came the sad

reply. "He was away from home for long stretches, he spoke a dozen impossible languages, he was secretive about what sort of work he did—I just wasn't paying attention."

"It amused everyone when he took you in as his ward," Minette said. "He was one of the coldest men Eb Scott ever hired—well, after Carson, who works for Cy Parks, that is." She chuckled. "But once you came along, all of a sudden Gabriel was smiling."

"He won't be anymore," Michelle said, feeling the pain to the soles of her feet.

"Give it time," was the older woman's advice. "First, you have some work to do."

"I know. I'm going to do everything in my power to prove him innocent. Whatever it takes," Michelle added firmly.

"That's more like it. And about the job," she replied. "Once you've proven that you aren't running away from an uncomfortable assignment, we'll have a place for you here. That's a promise."

"Thanks."

"You're welcome."

Michelle convinced Eb Scott to let her talk to his detective. It worked out well, because Dane Lassiter was actually in San Antonio for a seminar that week and he agreed to meet with her in a local restaurant.

He wasn't exactly what she'd expected. He was tall, dark-haired and dark-eyed, with an easygoing manner and a wife who was thirtysomething and very attractive. She, like Michelle, was blonde.

"We always go together when he has to give seminars." Tess laughed. "At least once I've had to chase a pursuing woman out of his room." She shook her head, sighing as she met her husband's amused gaze. "Well, after all, I know he's a dish. Why shouldn't other women notice?"

Michelle laughed with them, but her heart wasn't in it. There had been a snippet of news on television the night before, showing a camp of journalists on the road that led to the Brandons' Wyoming property. They were still trying to get Sara to talk to them. But this time they were met with a steely-eyed man Michelle recognized as Wofford Patterson, who was advising them to decamp before some of Sara's friends loosed a few bears on the property in a conservation project. Patterson had become Sara's personal protector and much more, after many years of antagonism.

"I've been watching the press reports on Brandon," Dane said, having guessed the train of her thoughts. "You watch six different reports and get six different stories."

"Yes," Michelle said sadly. "Not everyone tries for accuracy. And I can include myself in that company, because I should have gone the extra mile and presented the one dissenting opinion. It was easy to capitulate, because I didn't think I had any interest in the outcome," she added miserably.

Tess's pale eyes narrowed. "Mr. Brandon was your guardian."

She nodded. He was more, but she wasn't sharing that news with a virtual stranger. "I sold him out. I didn't mean to. I had no idea Angel was Gabriel. It was hard, going against a majority opinion. Everyone said he was guilty as sin. I saw the photographs of the women and children." Her face hardened. "It was easy to believe it, after that."

"I've seen similar things," Dane said, sipping black

coffee. "But I can tell you that things are rarely what they seem."

She told him about her contacts, and he took notes, getting names and telephone numbers and putting together a list of people to interview.

He put up his pen and notebook. "This is going to be a lot of help to the men who were blamed for the tragedy," he said finally. "There's a violent element in the country in question, dedicated to rooting out any hint of foreign influence, however beneficial. But at the same time, in their ranks are a few who see a way to quick profit, a way to fund their terrorism and inflict even more horror on our overseas personnel. This group that put your friend in the middle of the controversy is made up of a few money-hungry profiteers. Our State Department has worked very hard to try to stifle them. We have several oil corporations with offices there, and a good bit of our foreign oil is shipped from that country. We depend on the goodwill of the locals to keep the oil companies' officials and workers safe. The terrorists know that, and they see a way to make a quick profit through kidnappings and other attacks. Except that instead of holding people for ransom, they threaten violence if their demands aren't met. It's almost like a protection racket..."

"That's what he meant," Michelle said suddenly.

"Excuse me?"

"Eb Scott said, 'follow the money,'" she recalled.

"Eb's sharp. Yes, that's apparently what's behind all this. The terrorist leader wanted millions in bribes to protect oil company executives in his country. The brother-in-law of the leader was selling him out to our State Department. A lot of local men work for the oil companies and don't want any part of the terrorist's plans. It's a poor country, and the oil companies provide a secure living for the village. But nobody makes waves and gets away with it. The terrorist leader retaliated, in the worst possible way, and blamed it on Angel and his men—a way of protecting his own men, whom he ordered to kill his brother-in-law to keep him from talking. It was also a way of notifying foreigners that this is how any future attempts to bypass his authority would be handled."

"I'm not telling you anything you didn't already know," she said suddenly.

"I knew it. I couldn't prove it," he added. "But you've given me contacts who can back up the protester's story. I'll have my investigators check them out and our attorneys will take depositions that will hold up in court. It will give the State Department's representatives the leverage they need to deal with the terrorists. And it will provide our news media with a week of guaranteed stories," he added coldly.

She sighed. "I think I'm in the wrong business."

"Good reporters can do a lot of good in the world," Tess interrupted. "It's just that there's more profit in digging up dirt on people."

"Amen," Dane said.

"Well, if I can help dig Gabriel out of the hole I put him into, I'll be happy," Michelle told him. "It's little enough in the way of apology."

"If you hear anything else, through your sources, you can call me anytime," he told her.

"I'll remember."

Dane went to pay the check, against Michelle's protests.

Tess smiled at her. "You really care about the mercenary, don't you?" she asked.

"More than you know," Michelle replied. "He and his

sister sacrificed a lot for me. I'll never be able to pay them back. And now, this has happened...."

"At least you're trying to make up for it," she replied. "That's worth something."

"I hope it's worth enough. I'm grateful to you and your husband for meeting with me."

"It was a nice interlude between the rehashing of horrible cases." Tess laughed. "I work as a skip tracer, something Dane would never let me do before. My father planned to marry his mother, but they were killed in a wreck, so Dane became sort of responsible for me," she added surprisingly. "He wasn't very happy about it. We had a rocky road to the altar." She smiled. "But a son and a daughter later, we're very content."

"You don't look old enough to have two children." Michelle laughed. "Either of you."

"Thanks. But believe me, we are."

Dane was back, putting away his wallet. He handed Michelle a business card. "My cell's on there, as well as the office number."

"I'll cross my fingers, that our contacts can help you get Gabriel and his men off the hook," Michelle said.

His eyes narrowed. "I'm surprised that the national news media hasn't been camped on your doorstep," he remarked.

"Gabriel didn't advertise his involvement with me," she replied. "And nobody in Jacobsville, Texas, will tell them a thing, believe me."

He smiled. "I noticed the way the locals shut them out when they waltzed into town with their satellite trucks. Amazing, that the restaurants all ran out of food and the motels were all full and nobody had a single room to rent out at any price."

She smiled angelically. "I'm sure that was mostly true."

"They did try Comanche Wells, I hear," Dane added.

"Well, see, Comanche Wells doesn't have a restaurant or a motel at all."

"That explains it."

She went back to work, only to find her desk piled high with notes.

"Hey, Godfrey, can't you get your answering machine to work?" Murphy, one of the older reporters whose desk was beside hers, asked. "My old hands are too gnarled to take notes from all your darned callers."

"Sorry, Murph," she said. She was frowning when she noticed who the notes were from. "They want to send a limo for me and have me stay at the Plaza?" she exclaimed.

"What it is to be a celebrity," Murph shook his head. "Hey, there was this cool video that Brad Paisley did, about being a celebrity…!"

"I saw it. Thanks," she said, waving the notes at him. She picked up her purse and left the building, just avoiding her editor on the way out the door.

Apparently the news media had found somebody in Jacobsville who was willing to talk to them. She wondered with droll cynicism what the informant had been paid.

She discovered that if she agreed to do an exclusive interview with just one station, the others would have to leave her alone. Before she signed any papers, she spoke with an attorney and had him check out the agreement.

"It says that I agree to tell them my story," she said.

"Exactly," he replied.

She pursed her lips. "It doesn't specify which story."

"I think they'll assume it means the story they want to hear," he replied. "Although that's implied rather than stated."

"Ah."

"And I would advise caution when they ask you to name the person overseas whom your newspaper provided as a reference regarding the informer," he added. "That may be a protected source."

"I was hoping you'd notice that. It is a protected source."

He only smiled.

She sat down in front of the television cameras with a well-known, folksy interviewer who was calm, gentle and very intelligent. He didn't press her for details she couldn't give, and he understood that some sources of information that she had access to were protected.

"I understand from what you told our correspondent that you don't believe the men in question actually perpetrated the attack, which resulted in the deaths of several women and small children," he began.

"That's correct."

"Would you tell me why?"

"When I first broke the story, I went on the assumption that because the majority of the interviewees placed the blame on the American mercenaries, they must be guilty. There was, however, one conflicting opinion. A villager, whom I cannot name, said that extortion was involved and that money was demanded for the protection of foreign workers. When a relative of the extortionist threatened to go to the authorities and reveal the financial aspect, he and his family were brutally murdered as a warning. These murders were blamed on the Americans who had, in fact, been working for the government trying to uncover a nest of terrorists threatening American oil company employees there."

The interviewer was frowning. "Then the massacre was, in fact, retaliation for the villager's threat to expose the extortionist."

"That is my information, yes."

He studied a sheet of paper. "I see here that the newspaper which employs you used its own foreign sources to do interviews about this story."

"Those sources are also protected," Michelle replied. "I can't name them."

He pursed his lips and, behind his lenses, his blue eyes twinkled. "I understand. But I believe the same sources have been named, in the press, by attorneys for the men allegedly implicated by the international press for the atrocities."

She smiled. "I believe so."

"In which case," he added, "we have elicited permission to quote one of the sources. He has signed an affidavit, which is in the hands of our State Department. Please welcome Mr. David Arbuckle, who is liaison for the U.S. Department of State in Anasrah, which is at the center of this matter. Mr. Arbuckle, welcome."

"Thank you, Mr. Price," a pleasant-looking, middle-aged man replied. He was in a studio in Washington, D.C., his image provided via satellite.

"Now, from what Ms. Godfrey has told us—and we have validated her story—a terrorist cell had infiltrated the village in question and made threats against foreign nationals including ours. Is this true?"

"It is," Mr. Arbuckle said solemnly. "We're very grateful to Ms. Godfrey for bringing this matter to our attention. We were told that a group of mercenaries muscled their way into the village, demanding tribute and killed people when their demands were not met. This is a very different story than we were able to verify by speaking, under offer of protection, to other men in the same village."

He coughed, then continued, "We were able to ascertain that a terrorist cell with links to another notorious international organization was going to fund itself by extorting money from oil corporations doing business near the village. They were using the village itself for cover, posing as innocent tribesmen."

"Abominable," the host replied.

"Yes, killing innocents to prove a point is a particularly bloodthirsty manner in which to operate. The local people were terrified to say anything, after the massacre, although they felt very sad that innocent men were blamed for it. In fact, the so-called mercenaries had provided medical supplies and treatment for many children and elderly people and even helped buy food for them."

"A laudable outreach effort."

"Indeed," Mr. Arbuckle replied grimly. "Suffice it to say that we have used our influence to make sure that the terrorists no longer have a foothold in the village, and the international community has moved people in to assure the safety of the tribesmen who provided us with this information."

"Then the American mercenaries are being cleared of any involvement with the massacre?"

"I can assure you that they have been," Mr. Arbuckle replied. "We were provided with affidavits and other documents concerning the massacre by an American private detective working in concert with the mercenaries' attorneys. They were allowed to leave the country last night and are en route to a secure location while we deal with the terrorists in question. The terrorists responsible for the massacre will be brought to trial for the murders and held accountable. And the mercenaries will return to testify against them."

"I'm sure our viewers will be happy to hear that."

"We protect our people overseas," Mr. Arbuckle replied. "All of them. And in fact, the mercenaries in question were private contractors working for the United States government, not the sort of soldiers for hire that often involve themselves in foreign conflicts."

"Another surprise," Mr. Price said with a smile.

"In this day and time, we all have to be alert about our surroundings abroad," Mr. Arbuckle said. "We take care of our own," he added with a smile.

"Thank you for your time, Mr. Arbuckle."

"Thank you for yours, Mr. Price."

Mr. Price turned back to Michelle. "It was a very brave thing you did, Ms. Godfrey, going up against the weight of the international press to defend these men. I understand that you know some of them."

"I know Eb Scott, who runs an international school of counterterrorism," Michelle corrected, unwilling to say more. "He has great integrity. I can't imagine that any agents he trained would ever go against basic humanitarianism."

"He has a good advocate here." He chuckled.

"I learned a lesson from this, as well," she replied quietly. "That you don't discount the single small voice in the wilderness when you write a story that can cost lives and reputations. It is one I hope I never have to repeat." She paused. "I'd like to thank my editor for standing by me," she added, lying because he hadn't, "and for teaching me the worth of integrity in reporting."

Mr. Price named the newspaper in San Antonio and thanked her for appearing on his program.

* * *

Back in the office, her editor, Len Worthington, was ecstatic. "That was the nicest plug we ever got from anybody! Thanks, kid!" he told her, shaking her hand.

"You're welcome. Thanks for not firing me for messing up so badly."

"Hey, what are friends for?"

He'd never know, she thought, but she only smiled. She'd seen a side of journalism that left her feeling sick. It wasn't pretty.

She didn't try to call Sara again. The poor woman probably hadn't seen the program Michelle was on. It was likely that she was avoiding any sort of press coverage of what had happened. That wasn't hard anymore, because there was a new scandal topping the news now, and all the satellite trucks had gone in search of other prey. Michelle's phone had stopped ringing. There were no more notes on her desk, no more offers of limos and five-star hotels. She didn't mind at all.

She only hoped that one day Sara and Gabriel would forgive her. She went back to work on other stories, mostly political ones, and hoped that she'd never be in a position again where she'd have to sell out her nearest and dearest for a job. Not that she ever would. Nor would she have done it, if she'd had any idea who Gabriel really was.

Michelle had thought about asking Minette for a job again. She wasn't really happy living in the city and she cringed every time someone mentioned her name in connection with the past big news story.

She still hadn't heard from Gabriel or Sara. She didn't expect to. She'd hoped that they might contact her. But that was wishful thinking.

She now owned the home where her father and, before him, her grandparents had lived in Comanche Wells. She couldn't bear to drive the Jaguar that Gabriel and Sara had given her...driving it made her too sad. So she parked it at Gabriel's house and put the key in the mail slot. One day, she assumed, he'd return and see it. She bought a cute little VW bug, with which she could commute from Jacobsville to work in San Antonio. She moved back home.

At first, people were understandably a little standoffish. She was an outsider, even though she was born in Jacobs County. Perhaps they thought she was going to go all big-city on them and start poking her nose into local politics.

When she didn't do that, the tension began to ease a little. When she went into Barbara's Café to have lunch on Saturdays, people began to nod and smile at her. When she went grocery shopping in the local supermarket, the cashier actually talked to her. When she got gas at the local station, the attendant finally stopped asking for identification when she presented her credit card. Little by little, she was becoming part of Jacobs County again.

Carlie came to visit occasionally. She was happily married, and expecting her first child. They weren't as close as they had been, but it made Michelle feel good to know that her friend was settled and secure.

She only wished that she could be, settled and secure. But as months went by with no word of or from the Brandons, she gave up all hope that she might one day be forgiven for the things she'd written.

She knew that Sara had a whole new life in Wyoming from the cashier at the grocery store who had known her. Michelle didn't blame her for not wanting to come back to Texas. After all, she'd only lived in Comanche Wells as a favor to Gabriel, so that he could be Michelle's guardian.

Guardian no more, obviously. He'd given up that before, of course, when she turned twenty-one. But sometimes Michelle wished that she still had at least a relationship with him. She mourned what could have been, before she lost her way. Gabriel had assured her that they had a future. But that was before.

She was hanging out sheets in the yard, fighting the fierce autumn breeze to keep them from blowing away, when she heard a vehicle coming down the long road. It was odd, because nobody lived out this way except Michelle. It was Saturday. The next morning, she'd planned to go to church. She'd missed it for a couple of Sundays while she worked on a hot political story.

These days, not even the Reverend Blair came visiting much. She didn't visit other people, either. Her job occupied much of her time, because a reporter was always on call. But Michelle still attended services most Sundays.

So she stared at the truck as it went past the house. Its windows were tinted, and rolled up. It was a new truck, a very fancy one. Perhaps someone had bought the old Brandon place, she concluded, and went back to hanging up clothes. It made her sad to think that Gabriel would sell the ranch. But, after all, what would he need it for? He only had a manager there to care for it, so it wasn't as if he needed to keep it. He had other things to do.

She'd heard from Minette that Gabriel was part of an international police force now, one that Eb Scott had contracted with to provide security for those Middle Eastern oilmen who had played such a part in Gabriel's close call.

She wondered if he would ever come back to Comanche Wells. But she was fairly certain he wouldn't. Too many bad memories.

Chapter Twelve

Michelle finished hanging up her sheets in the cool breeze and went back into the house to fix herself a sandwich.

There were rumors at work that a big story was about to break involving an oil corporation and a terrorist group in the Middle East, one that might have local ties. Michelle, now her editor's favorite reporter for having mentioned him on TV, was given the assignment. It might, he hinted, involve some overseas travel. Not to worry, the paper would gladly pay her expenses.

She wondered what sort of mess she might get herself into this time, poking her nose into things she didn't understand. Well, it was a job, and she was lucky to even have one in this horrible economy.

She finished her sandwich and drank a cup of black coffee. For some reason she thought of Gabriel, and how much he'd enjoyed her coffee. She had to stop thinking about him. She'd almost cost him his life. She'd destroyed his peace of mind and Sara's, subjected them both to cameras and reporters and harassment. It was not really a surprise that they weren't speaking to her anymore. Even if she'd gone the last mile defending them, trying to make up for her lack of foresight, it didn't erase the damage she'd already done.

She was bored to death. The house was pretty. She'd made improvements—she'd redecorated Roberta's old room and had the whole place repainted. She'd put up new curtains and bought new furniture. But the house was cold and empty.

Back when her father was alive, it still held echoes of his parents, of him. Now, it was a reminder of old tragedies, most especially her father's death and Roberta's.

She carried her coffee into the living room and looked around her. She ought to sell it and move into an apartment in San Antonio. She didn't have a pet, not even a dog or cat, and the livestock her father had owned were long gone. She had nothing to hold her here except a sad attachment to the past, to dead people.

But there was something that kept her from letting go. She knew what it was, although she didn't want to remember. It was Gabriel. He'd eaten here, slept here, comforted her here. It was warm with memories that no other dwelling place would ever hold.

She wondered if she couldn't just photograph the rooms and blow up the photos, make posters of them, and sacrifice the house.

Sure, she thought hollowly. Of course she could.

She finished her coffee and turned on the television. Same old stories. Same programs with five minutes of commercials for every one minute of programming. She switched it off. These days she only watched DVDs or streamed movies from internet websites. She was too antsy to sit through a hundred commercials every half hour.

She wondered why people put up with it. If everyone stopped watching television, wouldn't the advertisers be forced to come up with alternatives that compromised a bit more? Sure. And cows would start flying any day.

That reminded her of the standing joke she'd had with Grier and Gabriel about cows being abducted by aliens, and it made her sad.

Outside, she heard the truck go flying past her house. It didn't even slow down. Must be somebody looking at Gabriel's house. She wondered if he'd put it on the market without bothering to put a for-sale sign out front. Why not? He had no real ties here. He'd probably moved up to Wyoming to live near Sara.

She went into the kitchen, put her coffee cup in the sink, and went back to her washing.

She wore a simple beige skirt and a short-sleeved beige sweater to church with pretty high heels and a purse to match. She left her hair long, down her back, and used only a trace of makeup on her face.

She'd had ample opportunities for romance, but all those years she'd waited for Gabriel, certain that he was going to love her one day, that she had a future with him. Now that future was gone. She knew that one day, she'd have to decide if she really wanted to be nothing more than a career woman with notoriety and money taking the place of a husband and children and a settled life.

There was nothing wrong with ambition. But the few career women she'd known seemed empty somehow, as if they presented a happy face to the world but that it was like a mask, hiding the insecurities and loneliness that accompanied a demanding lifestyle. What would it be like to grow old, with no family around you, with only friends and acquaintances and business associates to mark the holidays? Would it make up for the continuity of the next generation and the generation after that, of seeing your features reproduced down through your children and grandchildren and great-grandchildren? Would it make up for laughing little voices and busy little hands, and soft kisses on your cheek at bedtime?

That thought made her want to cry. She'd never thought too much about kids during her school days, but when Gabriel had kissed her and talked about a future, she'd dreamed of having his children. It had been a hunger unlike anything she'd ever known.

She had to stop tormenting herself. She had to come to grips with the world the way it was, not the way she wanted it to be. She was a grown woman with a promising career. She had to look ahead, not behind her.

She slid into her usual pew, listened to Reverend Blair's sermon and sang along with the choir as they repeated the chorus of a well-loved old hymn. Sometime during the offering, she was aware of a tingling sensation, as if someone were watching her. She laughed silently. Now she was getting paranoid.

As the service ended, and they finished singing the final hymn, as the benediction sounded in Reverend Blair's clear, deep voice, she continued to have the sensation that someone was watching her.

Slowly, as her pew filed out into the aisle, she glanced toward the back of the church. But there was no one there, no one looking at her. What a strange sensation.

* * *

Reverend Blair shook her hand and smiled at her. "It's nice to have you back, Miss Godfrey," he teased.

She smiled back. "Rub it in. I had a nightmare of a political story to follow. I spent so much time on it that I'm thinking I may run for public office myself. By now, I know exactly what not to do to get elected," she confided with a chuckle.

"I know what you mean. It was a good story."

"Thanks."

"See you next week."

"I hope." She crossed her fingers. He just smiled.

She walked to her car and clicked the smart key to unlock it when she felt, rather than saw, someone behind her.

She turned and her heart stopped in her chest. She looked up into liquid black eyes in a tanned, hard face that looked as if it had never known a smile.

She swallowed. She wanted to say so many things. She wanted to apologize. She wanted to cry. She wanted to throw herself into his arms and beg him to hold her, comfort her, forgive her. But she did none of those things. She just looked up at him hopelessly, with dead eyes that looked as if they had never held joy.

His square chin lifted. His eyes narrowed on her face. "You've lost weight."

She shrugged. "One of the better consequences of my profession," she said quietly. "How are you, Gabriel?"

"I've been better."

She searched his eyes. "How's Sara?"

"Getting back to normal."

She nodded. She swallowed again and dropped her eyes to his chest. It was hard to find something to say that didn't involve apologies or explanations or pleas for forgiveness.

The silence went on for so long that she could hear pieces of conversation from other churchgoers. She could hear the traffic on the highway, the sound of children playing in some yard nearby. She could hear the sound of her own heartbeat.

This was destroying her. She clicked the key fob again deliberately. "I have to go," she said softly.

"Sure."

He moved back so that she could open the door and get inside. She glanced at him with sorrow in her face, but she averted her eyes so that it didn't embarrass him. She didn't want him to feel guilty. She was the one who should feel that emotion. In the end she couldn't meet his eyes or even wave. She just started the car and drove away.

Well, at least the first meeting was over with, she told herself later. It hadn't been quite as bad as she'd expected. But it had been rough. She felt like crying, but her eyes were dry. Some pain was too deep to be eased by tears, she thought sadly.

She changed into jeans and a red T-shirt and went out on the front porch to water her flowers while a TV dinner microwaved itself to perfection in the kitchen.

Her flowers were going to be beautiful when they bloomed, she decided, smiling as they poked their little heads up through the dirt in an assortment of ceramic pots all over the wooden floor.

She had three pots of chrysanthemums and one little bonsai tree named Fred. Gabriel had given it to her when she first moved in with them, a sort of welcome present. It was a tiny fir tree with a beautiful curving trunk and feathery limbs. She babied it, bought it expensive fertilizer, read books on how to keep it healthy and worried herself to death that it might accidentally die if she forgot to water it. That hadn't happened, of course, but she loved it dearly. Of all the things Gabriel had given her, and there had been a lot, this was her favorite. She left it outside until the weather grew too cold, then she carried it inside protectively.

The Jaguar had been wonderful. But she'd still been driving it when she did the story that almost destroyed Gabriel's life and after that, she could no longer bear to sit in it. The memories had been killing her.

She missed the Jag. She missed Gabriel more. She wondered why he'd come back. Probably to sell the house, she decided, to cut his last tie with Comanche Wells. If he was working for an international concern, it wasn't likely that he'd plan to come back here. He'd see the Jag in the driveway, she thought, and understand why she'd given it back. At least, she hoped he would.

That thought, that he might leave Comanche Wells forever, was really depressing. She watered Fred, put down the can, and went back into the house. It didn't occur to her to wonder what he'd been doing at her church.

When she went into the kitchen to take her dinner out of the microwave, a dark-haired man was sitting at the table sipping coffee. There were two cups, one for him and one for her. The dinner was sitting on a plate with a napkin and silverware beside it.

He glanced up as she came into the room. "It's getting cold," he said simply.

She stood behind her chair, just staring at him, frowning.

He raised an eyebrow as he studied her shirt. "You

know, most people who wore red shirts on the original *Star Trek* ended up dead."

She cocked her head. "And you came all this way to give me fashion advice?"

He managed a faint smile. "Not really." He sipped coffee. He let out a long breath. "It's been a long time, Michelle."

She nodded. Slowly, she pulled out the chair and sat down. The TV dinner had the appeal of mothballs. She pushed it aside and sipped the black coffee he'd put at her place. He still remembered how she took it, after all this time.

She ran her finger around the rim. "I learned a hard lesson," she said after a minute. "Reporting isn't just about presenting the majority point of view."

He lifted his eyes to hers. "Life teaches very hard lessons."

"Yes, it does." She drew in a breath. "I guess you're selling the house."

His eyebrows lifted. "Excuse me?"

"I saw a truck go out there yesterday. And I read that you're working with some international police force now. So since Sara's living in Wyoming, I assumed you'd probably be moving up there near her. For when you're home in the States, I mean."

"I'd considered it," he said after a minute. He sipped more coffee.

She wondered if her heart could fall any deeper into her chest. She wondered how in the world he'd gotten into the house so silently. She wondered why he was there in the first place. Was he saying goodbye?

"Did you find the keys to the Jag?" she asked.

"Yes. You didn't want to keep it?"

She swallowed hard. "Too many bad memories, of what I did to you and Sara," she confessed heavily.

He shook his head. After a minute, he stared at her bent head. "I don't think you've really looked at me once," he said finally.

She managed a tight smile. "It's very hard to do that, after all the trouble I caused you," she said. "I rehearsed it, you know. Saying I was sorry. Working up all sorts of ways to apologize. But there really isn't a good way to say it."

"People make mistakes."

"The kind I made could have buried you." She said it tautly, fighting tears. It was harder than she'd imagined. She forced down the rest of the coffee. "Look, I've got things to do," she began, standing, averting her face so he couldn't see her eyes.

"Ma belle," he whispered, in a voice so tender that her control broke the instant she heard it. She burst into tears.

He scooped her up in his arms and kissed her so hungrily that she just went limp, arching up to him, so completely his that she wouldn't have protested anything he wanted to do to her.

"So it's like that, is it?" he whispered against her soft, trembling mouth. "Anything I want? Anything at all?"

"Anything," she wept.

"Out of guilt?" he asked, and there was an edge to his tone now.

She opened her wet eyes and looked into his. "Out of…love," she choked.

"Love."

"Go ahead. Laugh…"

He buried his face in her throat. "I thought I'd lost you for good," he breathed huskily. "Standing there at your car, looking so defeated, so depressed that you couldn't even meet my eyes. I thought, I'll have to leave, there's nothing left, nothing there except guilt and sorrow. And then I decided to have one last try, to come here and talk to you. You walked into the room and every single thing you felt was there, right there, in your eyes when you looked at me. And I knew, then, that it wasn't over at all. It was only beginning."

Her arms tightened around his neck. Her eyes were pouring with hot tears. "I loved you…so much," she choked. "Sara said you never wanted to see me again. She hated me. I knew you must hate me, too…!"

He kissed the tears away. He sat down on the sofa with Michelle in his lap and curled her into his chest. "Sara has a quick, hot temper. She loses it, and it's over. She's sorry that she was so brutal with you. She was frightened and upset and the media was hunting her. She's had other problems as well, that you don't know about. But she's ashamed that she took it all out on you, blamed you for something you didn't even do deliberately." He lifted his head and smoothed the long, damp hair away from her cheek. "She wanted to apologize, but she's too ashamed to call you."

"That's why?" she whispered. "I thought I would never see her again. Or you."

"That would never happen," he said gently. "You're part of us."

She bit her lower lip. "I sold you out…!"

"You did not. You sold out a mercenary named Angel, someone you didn't know, someone you thought had perpetrated a terrible crime against innocent women and children," he said simply. He brushed his mouth over her wet eyes. "You would never have sold me out in a million years, even if you had thought I was guilty as sin."

He lifted his head and looked into her eyes. "Because you love me. You love me enough to forgive anything, even murder."

The tears poured out even hotter. She couldn't stop crying.

He wrapped her up close, turned her under him on the sofa, slid between her long legs and began to kiss her with anguished hunger. The kisses grew so long and so hard and so hot that she trembled and curled her legs around the back of his, urging him into greater intimacy, pleading with him to ease the tension that was putting her young body on the rack.

"If you don't stop crying," he threatened huskily, "this is going to end badly."

"No, it isn't. You want to," she whispered, kissing his throat.

"Yes, I do," he replied deeply. "But you're going to need a lot of time that I can't give you when I'm out of control," he murmured darkly. "You won't enjoy it."

"Are you sure?" she whispered.

He lifted his head. His eyes were hot and hungry on her body. His hands had pushed up the red shirt and the bra, and he was staring at her pert, pretty breasts with aching need. "I am absolutely sure," he managed.

"Oh."

The single word and the wide-eyed, hopeless look in her eyes broke the tension and he started laughing. "That's it? 'Oh'?"

She laughed, too. "Well, I read a lot and I watch movies, but it's not quite the same thing…"

"Exactly."

He forced himself to roll off her. "If you don't mind, could you pull all this back down?" he asked, indicating her breasts. He averted his eyes. "And I'll try deep breaths and mental imagery of snow-covered hills."

"Does it work?"

"Not really."

She pulled down her shirt and glanced at him with new knowledge of him and herself, and smiled.

"That's a smug little look," he accused.

"I like knowing I can throw you off balance," she said with a wicked grin.

"I'll enjoy letting you do it, but not until we're used to each other," he replied. He pulled her close. "The first time has to be slow and easy," he whispered, brushing his mouth over hers. "So that it doesn't hurt so much."

"If you can knock me off balance, I won't care if it hurts," she pointed out.

His black eyes twinkled. "I'll remember that."

She lay back on the sofa and looked up at him with wide, wondering eyes. "I thought it was all over," she whispered. "That I had nothing left, nothing to live for..."

"I felt the same way," he returned, solemn and quiet. "Thank God I decided to make one more attempt to get through to you."

She smiled gently. "Fate."

He smiled back. "Yes. Fate."

"Where are you going? Come back here." She pulled him back down.

He pursed his lips. "We need to discuss things vertically, not horizontally."

"I'm not going to seduce you, honest. I have something very serious I need to talk to you about."

"Okay. What?"

She pursed her own lips and her eyes twinkled. "Cow abductions."

He burst out laughing.

* * *

They were married in the Methodist church two weeks later by Reverend Blair. Michelle wore a conventional white gown with lace inserts and a fingertip veil, which Gabriel lifted to kiss her for the first time as his wife. In the audience were more mercenaries and ex-military and feds than anyone locally had seen in many a year.

Eb Scott and his wife, along with Dr. Micah Steele and Callie, and Cy Parks and Lisa, were all in the front row with Minette Carson and her husband Hayes. Carlie and her husband were there, too.

There was a reception in the fellowship hall and Jacobsville police chief Cash Grier kept looking around restlessly.

"Is something going on that we should know about?" Gabriel asked with a grin.

"Just waiting for the riot to break out."

"What riot?" Michelle asked curiously.

"You know, somebody says something, somebody else has too much to drink and takes offense, blows are exchanged, police are called in to break up the altercation…"

"Chief Grier, just how many riots at weddings have you seen?" she wanted to know.

"About half a dozen," he said.

"Well, I can assure you, there won't be any here," Michelle said. "Because there's no booze!"

Cash gaped at her. "No booze?"

"No."

"Well, damn," he said, glowering at her.

"Why do you say that?" she asked.

"How can you have altercations without booze?" He threw up his hands. "And I had so looked forward to a little excitement around here!"

"I could throw a punch at Hayes," Gabriel offered, grinning at the sheriff. "But then he'd have to arrest me, and Michelle would spend our honeymoon looking for bail bondsmen...."

Cash chuckled. "Just kidding. I like the occasional quiet wedding." He leaned forward. "When you're not busy, you might want to ask Blake Kemp about *his* wedding reception, though," he added gleefully. "Jacobsville will never forget that one, I swear!"

Michelle lay trembling in Gabriel's arms, hot and damp in the aftermath of something so turbulent and thrilling that she knew she could live on the memory of it for the rest of her life.

"I believe the chief wanted a little excitement?" She laughed hoarsely. "I don't think anyone could top this. Ever."

He trailed his fingers up her body, lingering tenderly on a distended nipple. He stroked it until she arched and gasped. "I don't think so, either." He bent his head and slipped his lips over the dusky peak, teasing it until it grew even harder and she shivered. He suckled it, delighting in the sounds that came out of her throat.

"You like that, do you?" he whispered. He moved over her. "How about this?"

"Oh...yes," she choked. "Yes!"

He slid a hand under her hips and lifted her into the slow penetration of his body, moving restlessly as she accepted him, arched to greet him, shivered again as she felt the slow, hungry depth of his envelopment.

"It's easier now," he whispered. "Does it hurt?"

"I haven't...noticed yet," she managed, shuddering as he moved on her.

He chuckled.

"I was afraid," she confessed in a rush of breath.

"I know."

She clung to him as the rhythm lifted her, teased her body into contortions of pure, exquisite pleasure. "I can't believe...I was afraid!"

His hips moved from side to side and she made a harsh, odd little cry that was echoed in the convulsion of her hips.

"Yes," he purred. "I can make you so hungry that you'll do anything to get me closer, can't I, *ma belle?*"

"Any...thing," she agreed.

He ground his teeth together. "It works...both ways... too," he bit off. He groaned harshly as the pleasure bit into him, arched him down into her as the rhythm grew hard and hot and deep. He felt his heartbeat in his head, slamming like a hammer as he drove into her welcoming body, faster and harder and closer until suddenly, like a storm breaking, a silver shaft of pleasure went through him like a spear, lifting him above her in an arch so brittle that he thought he might shatter into a thousand pieces.

"Like...dying," he managed as the pleasure took him.

She clung to him, too involved to even manage a reply, lifting and pleading, digging her nails into his hard back as she welcomed the hard, heavy push of his body, welcomed the deep, aching tension that grew and swelled and finally burst like rockets going off inside her.

She cried out helplessly, sobbing, as the ecstasy washed over her like the purest form of pleasure imaginable and then, just as quickly, was gone. Gone. Gone!

They clung together, damp with sweat, sliding against each other in the aftermath, holding on to the echoes of the exquisite satisfaction that they'd shared.

"Remind me to tell you one day how rare it is for two people to find completion at the same time," he whispered, sliding his mouth over her soft, yielding body. "Usually, the woman takes a long time, and the man only finds his satisfaction when hers is over."

She lifted an eyebrow. "And you would know this, how?" she began.

He lifted his head and looked into her eyes with a rakish grin. "Oh, from the videos I watched and the books I read and the other guys I listened to...."

"Is that so?" she mused, with a suspicious look.

He kissed her accusing eyes shut. "It was long before I knew you," he whispered. "And after the first day I saw you, sitting in the road waiting for me to run over you, there was no one. Ever."

Her eyes flew open. "Wh-what?"

He brushed the hair from her cheeks. "I knew then that I would love you one day, forever," he said quietly. "So there were no other women."

Her face flushed. "Gabriel," she whispered, overcome.

He kissed her tenderly. "The waiting was terrible," he groaned. "I thought I might die of it, waiting until you grew up, until you knew something of the world and men so that I didn't rob you of that experience." He lifted his head. "Always, I worried that you might find a younger man and fall in love..."

She put her fingers over his chiseled mouth. "I loved you from the day I met you," she whispered. "When I stared at you, that day in town with my grandfather, before I was even sixteen." She touched his cheek with her fingertips. "I knew, too, that there could never be anyone else."

He nibbled her fingers. "So sweet, the encounter after all the waiting," he whispered.

"Sweeter than honey," she agreed, her eyes warm and soft on his face.

"There's just one thing," he murmured.

She raised her eyebrows.

He opened a drawer and pulled out an item that he'd placed there earlier. An item that they'd forgotten to use.

She just smiled.

After a minute, he smiled back and dropped the item right back into the drawer.

Sara was overjoyed. "I can't wait to come down there and see you both," she exclaimed. "But you've only been married six weeks," she added.

Gabriel was facing the computer with Michelle at his side, holding her around the waist, his big hands resting protectively over her slightly swollen belly as they talked on Skype with Sara in Wyoming. "We were both very sure that it was what we wanted," he said simply.

"Well, I'm delighted," Sara said. She smiled. "The only way I could be more delighted is if it was me who was pregnant. But, that will come with time," she said complacently, and smiled. "I'm only sorry I couldn't be at the wedding," she added quietly. "I was very mean to you, Michelle. I couldn't face you, afterward."

"I understood," Michelle said gently. "You're my sister. Really my sister now," she added with a delighted laugh. "We're going to get a place near yours in Wyoming so that we can be nearby when the baby comes."

"I can't wait!"

"Neither can I," Michelle said. "We'll talk to you soon."

"Very soon." Sara smiled and cut the connection.

"Have you ever told her?" Michelle asked after a minute, curling up in Gabriel's lap.

He kissed her. "We did just tell her, my love…"

"Not about the baby," she protested. "About Wolf. About who he really is."

"You mean, her gaming partner for the past few years?" He grinned. "That's a story for another day."

"If you say so."

He kissed her. "I do say so. And now, how about a nice pickle and some vanilla ice cream?"

Her eyebrows lifted. "You know, that sounds delicious!"

He bent his head and kissed the little bump below her waist. "He's going to be extraordinary," he whispered.

"Yes. Like his dad," she replied with her heart in her eyes.

And they both grinned.

* * * * *

In November, from Harlequin HQN,
don't miss Sara and Wolf's romance in
WYOMING STRONG
by Diana Palmer.
Available in stores and through e-tailers
wherever books are sold.

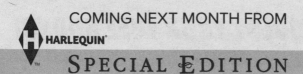

REQUEST YOUR FREE BOOKS!
2 FREE NOVELS PLUS 2 FREE GIFTS!

HARLEQUIN®

SPECIAL EDITION

Life, Love & Family

YES! Please send me 2 FREE Harlequin® Special Edition novels and my 2 FREE gifts (gifts are worth about $10). After receiving them, if I don't wish to receive any more books, I can return the shipping statement marked "cancel." If I don't cancel, I will receive 6 brand-new novels every month and be billed just $4.74 per book in the U.S. or $5.24 per book in Canada. That's a savings of at least 14% off the cover price! It's quite a bargain! Shipping and handling is just 50¢ per book in the U.S. and 75¢ per book in Canada.* I understand that accepting the 2 free books and gifts places me under no obligation to buy anything. I can always return a shipment and cancel at any time. Even if I never buy another book, the two free books and gifts are mine to keep forever.

235/335 HDN F45Y

Name	(PLEASE PRINT)	
Address		Apt. #
City	State/Prov.	Zip/Postal Code

Signature (if under 18, a parent or guardian must sign)

Mail to the Harlequin® Reader Service:
IN U.S.A.: P.O. Box 1867, Buffalo, NY 14240-1867
IN CANADA: P.O. Box 609, Fort Erie, Ontario L2A 5X3

Want to try two free books from another line?
Call 1-800-873-8635 or visit www.ReaderService.com.

* Terms and prices subject to change without notice. Prices do not include applicable taxes. Sales tax applicable in N.Y. Canadian residents will be charged applicable taxes. Offer not valid in Quebec. This offer is limited to one order per household. Not valid for current subscribers to Harlequin Special Edition books. All orders subject to credit approval. Credit or debit balances in a customer's account(s) may be offset by any other outstanding balance owed by or to the customer. Please allow 4 to 6 weeks for delivery. Offer available while quantities last.

Your Privacy—The Harlequin® Reader Service is committed to protecting your privacy. Our Privacy Policy is available online at www.ReaderService.com or upon request from the Harlequin Reader Service.

We make a portion of our mailing list available to reputable third parties that offer products we believe may interest you. If you prefer that we not exchange your name with third parties, or if you wish to clarify or modify your communication preferences, please visit us at www.ReaderService.com/consumerschoice or write to us at Harlequin Reader Service Preference Service, P.O. Box 9062, Buffalo, NY 14269. Include your complete name and address.

HSE13R

***

She exhaled noisily and collapsed on the other end of the couch. "Casey—"

"I just wanted to see you."

She slowly closed her mouth, absorbing that. Her fingers tightened around the glass. She could have offered him one. He'd been the one to introduce her to that particular winery in the first place. The first time she'd invited him to her place after they'd moved their relationship into the "benefits" category, he'd brought a bottle of wine.

She'd been wholly unnerved by it and told him they weren't dating—just mutually filling a need—and to save the empty romantic gestures.

He hadn't brought a bottle of wine ever again.

She shook off the memory.

He was here now, in her home, uninvited, and she'd be smart to remember that. "Why?"

He pushed off the couch and prowled around her living room. He'd always been intense. But she'd never really seen him *tense*. And she realized she was seeing it now.

She slowly sat forward and set her glass on the coffee table, watching him. "Casey, what's wrong?"

He shoved his fingers through his hair, not answering. Instead, he stopped in front of a photo collage on the wall above her narrow bookcase that Julia had given her last Christmas. "You going to go out with him again?"

Something ached inside her. "Probably," she admitted after a moment.

"He's a good guy," he muttered. "A little straightlaced, but otherwise okay."

She didn't know what was going on with him. But she suddenly felt like crying, and Jane wasn't a person who cried. "Casey."

"You could do worse." Then he gave her a tight smile and walked out of the living room into the kitchen. A second later, she heard the sound of her back door opening and closing.

He couldn't have left her more bewildered if he'd tried.

***

Find out what happens next in
New York Times *bestselling author Allison Leigh's*
A WEAVER CHRISTMAS GIFT, the latest in
THE RETURN TO THE DOUBLE C *miniseries.*

Available November 2014 from
Harlequin® Special Edition.

HARLEQUIN®

SPECIAL EDITION

Life, Love and Family

Coming in November 2014

THE SOLDIER'S HOLIDAY HOMECOMING

by *USA TODAY* bestselling author

Judy Duarte

Sergeant Joe Wilcox is back where he never expected to be—Brighton Valley, which he left long ago. He's in town because he promised to deliver a letter for a fellow marine to Chloe Dawson, who broke his late pal's heart. But before he can do so, Joe is struck by a car and gets temporary amnesia. Joe can't remember who he is, but he's intrigued by the lovely Chloe. Can the soldier and his sweetheart find happily-ever-after just in time for Christmas?

Don't miss the latest edition of the *Return to Brighton Valley* **miniseries!**

Available wherever books and ebooks are sold.

www.Harlequin.com

HSE65849

HARLEQUIN®

SPECIAL EDITION

Life, Love and Family

A Celebration Christmas

Don't miss the latest in the
Celebrations Inc. miniseries,
by reader-favorite author
Nancy Robards Thompson!

It's almost Christmas, but Dr. Cullen Dunlevy
has his hands full. Recently named caretaker for his
late best friend's children, Cullen needs help,
so he hires the lovely Lily Palmer as a nanny.
Lily believes wholeheartedly in the power of love
and is determined to show her boss what it means
to have holiday spirit. The dashing doctor might
just have a family under his tree for Christmas!

Available November 2014
wherever books and ebooks are sold.

Love the Harlequin book
you just read?

Your opinion matters.

Review this book on your favorite
book site, review site, blog or your own
social media properties and share
your opinion with other readers!